PENGUIN CLASSICS
Maigret at Picratt's

'I love reading Simenon. He makes me think of Chekhov'
— William Faulkner

'A truly wonderful writer . . . marvellously readable – lucid,
simple, absolutely in tune with the world he creates'
— Muriel Spark

'Few writers have ever conveyed with such a sure touch, the
bleakness of human life' — A. N. Wilson

'One of the greatest writers of the twentieth century . . .
Simenon was unequalled at making us look inside, though
the ability was masked by his brilliance at absorbing us
obsessively in his stories' — *Guardian*

'A novelist who entered his fictional world as if he were part
of it' — Peter Ackroyd

'The greatest of all, the most genuine novelist we have had
in literature' — André Gide

'Superb . . . The most addictive of writers . . . A unique teller
of tales' — *Observer*

'The mysteries of the human personality are revealed in all
their disconcerting complexity' — Anita Brookner

'A writer who, more than any other crime novelist, combined
a high literary reputation with popular appeal'
— P. D. James

'A supreme writer . . . Unforgettable vividness' – *Independent*

'Compelling, remorseless, brilliant' — John Gray

'Extraordinary masterpieces of the twentieth century'
— John Banville

ABOUT THE AUTHOR

Georges Simenon was born on 12 February 1903 in Liège, Belgium, and died in 1989 in Lausanne, Switzerland, where he had lived for the latter part of his life. Between 1931 and 1972 he published seventy-five novels and twenty-eight short stories featuring Inspector Maigret.

Simenon always resisted identifying himself with his famous literary character, but acknowledged that they shared an important characteristic:

> My motto, to the extent that I have one, has been noted often enough, and I've always conformed to it. It's the one I've given to old Maigret, who resembles me in certain points . . . 'understand and judge not'.

Penguin is publishing the entire series of Maigret novels.

GEORGES SIMENON

Maigret at Picratt's

Translated by WILLIAM HOBSON

PENGUIN BOOKS

PENGUIN CLASSICS

UK | USA | Canada | Ireland | Australia
India | New Zealand | South Africa

Penguin Books is part of the Penguin Random House group of companies
whose addresses can be found at global.penguinrandomhouse.com

Penguin
Random House
UK

First published in French as *Maigret au Picratt's* by Presses de la Cité 1951
This translation first published 2016
013

Copyright © Georges Simenon Limited, 1951
Translation copyright © William Hobson, 2016
GEORGES SIMENON ® Simenon.tm
MAIGRET ® Georges Simenon Limited
All rights reserved

Set in DanteMT Std 12.5/15pt
Typeset in India by Thomson Digital Pvt Ltd, Noida, Delhi
Printed and bound in Great Britain by Clays Ltd, Elcograf S.p.A.

ISBN: 978-0-241-24028-1

www.greenpenguin.co.uk

Maigret at Picratt's

1.

For Officer Jussiaume, whose beat took him to the same places at almost exactly the same time every night, these comings and goings were such a part of his routine that he registered them unconsciously, a little as people living next to a station register the arrivals and departures of trains.

It was sleeting, and Jussiaume had taken shelter for a moment in a doorway on the corner of Rue Fontaine and Rue Pigalle. Picratt's red sign was one of the few in the neighbourhood still to be on, its reflection leaving what looked like splashes of blood on the wet cobbles.

It was Monday, a slack day in Montmartre. Jussiaume could have told you the order in which most of the nightclubs had shut. He saw Picratt's neon sign go out in its turn, and the proprietor, short and stout, a beige raincoat over his dinner-jacket, came out on to the pavement to wind down the shutters with the crank.

A figure – a street urchin, it looked like – slid along the walls and went down Rue Pigalle towards Rue Blanche. Then two men, one of them with a saxophone case under his arm, headed up towards Place Clichy.

Almost immediately another man set off towards Carrefour Saint-Georges, his overcoat collar turned up.

Officer Jussiaume didn't know their names, he barely knew their faces, but these figures, and hundreds of others, meant something to him.

He knew that a woman would come out next, wearing a light-coloured, very short fur coat, perched on exaggeratedly high heels, and break into a very fast walk as if she were afraid to find herself alone on the street at four in the morning. She only had a hundred metres to go to get to her apartment block. She had to ring the bell, because at that time of night the front door was locked.

Finally the last two women came out together, as they always did, walked to the corner of the street, talking in low voices, and went their separate ways a few metres from where he was standing. One of them, the older, taller one, strutted back up Rue Pigalle to Rue Lepic, where he had sometimes seen her go into her apartment block. The other hesitated, looked at him as if she wanted to talk to him, and then, instead of going down Rue Notre-Dame-de-Lorette, as she should have, made for the café-tabac on the corner of Rue de Douai, which still had its lights on.

She had been drinking by the looks of it. She was bareheaded. He could see her golden hair gleam when she went under the streetlights. She walked slowly, stopping from time to time as if she were talking to herself.

'Coffee, Arlette?' the café owner asked familiarly.

'With a shot.'

The characteristic smell of rum heated by coffee immediately filled the air. Two or three men were drinking at the bar, but she didn't look at them.

The owner said later that she had seemed very tired.

That was probably why she had a second coffee with a double shot of rum, and her hand fumbled a little as she took the coins out of her bag.

'Good night.'

'Good night.'

Officer Jussiaume saw her head back his way, and, as she came down the street, her gait was even less steady than when she had gone up. When she drew level with him, she noticed him in the shadows, turned to face him and said:

'I want to make a statement at the station.'

'Easily done. You know where it is.'

It was almost directly opposite, more or less behind Picratt's, in Rue de La Rochefoucauld. From where they were standing, both of them could see the blue light and the police bicycles lined up against its wall.

He thought she wouldn't go at first. But then he saw her crossing the road and entering the station.

It was 4.30 when she walked into the dimly lit office, which was empty except for Sergeant Simon and a young trainee officer.

'I want to make a statement,' she repeated.

'I'm listening, sweetheart,' replied Simon, who had been in the area for twenty years and knew its ins and outs.

She was wearing a lot of make-up, which had run a little, and a black satin dress under a faux mink coat. She staggered slightly and held on to the handrail dividing the police officers from the public area.

'It's about a crime.'

'There's been a crime committed?'

A large electric clock hung on the wall, and she gazed at it as if the position of the hands held some significance.

'I don't know if it has been committed.'

'Then it's not a crime,' the sergeant said, winking at his young colleague.

'It's probably been committed. I'm sure it's been committed.'

'Who told you?'

She seemed to be laboriously following her train of thought.

'The two men, just now.'

'Which men?'

'Customers. I work at Picratt's.'

'I thought I'd seen you somewhere. You're the one who gets her clothes off, aren't you?'

The sergeant hadn't seen Picratt's floorshows, but he passed the club every morning and evening and had seen the large-format photograph in the window of the woman standing in front of him, as well as the smaller photographs of the other two dancers.

'So, just like that, some customers told you about a crime, did they?'

'They didn't tell me.'

'Who did they tell?'

'They were talking about it among themselves.'

'And you were listening?'

'Yes. I didn't hear everything. There was a partition between us.'

This was something else Sergeant Simon understood. When you walked past the club as it was being cleaned, the door would be open. You could see a dark room, entirely painted red, with a glossy dance-floor and tables along the walls, which were partitioned off into booths.

'Go on, then. When was this?'

'Tonight. About two hours ago. That's right, it must have been two in the morning. I'd only done my act once.'

'What did the two customers say?'

'The older one said he was going to kill the countess.'

'Which countess?'

'I don't know.'

'When?'

'Today, probably.'

'He wasn't afraid you'd hear?'

'He didn't know I was the other side of the partition.'

'Were you on your own?'

'No. With another customer.'

'Who you knew?'

'Yes.'

'Who was that?'

'I only know his first name. He's called Albert.'

'Did he hear too?'

'I don't think so.'

'Why not?'

'Because he was holding my hands and talking to me.'

'About how he loved you?'

'Yes.'

'And you were listening to what was being said in the next booth? Can you remember their exact words?'

'Not the exact ones.'

'Are you drunk?'

'I have been drinking, but I still know what I'm talking about.'

'Do you drink like this every night?'

'Not this much.'

'Did you drink with Albert?'

'We just had a bottle of champagne. I didn't want him to splash out.'

'He's not rich?'

'He's a young man.'

'Is he in love with you?'

'Yes. He'd like me to leave the club.'

'So, you were with him when the two customers came in and sat down in the next booth.'

'That's right.'

'You didn't see them?'

'I saw them later, from behind, as they left.'

'Did they stay for a long time?'

'Maybe half an hour.'

'Did they have champagne with the women you work with?'

'No. I think they ordered brandy.'

'And they started talking about the countess right away?'

'Not right away. At the beginning, I didn't pay any attention. The first thing I heard was something like: "You understand, she's still got most of her jewellery, but at the rate she's going it won't be for long."'

'What sort of voice?'

'A man's voice. A middle-aged man's. When they left, I saw that one of them was short and burly, with grey hair. It must have been him.'

'Why?'

'Because the other one was younger, and it wasn't a young man's voice.'

'How was he dressed?'

'I didn't notice. I think he was wearing dark clothes, maybe black.'

'Did they leave their coats in the cloakroom?'

'I suppose.'

'So, he said the countess still had most of her jewellery but at the rate she was going it wouldn't be for long?'

'That's right.'

'What did he say about killing her?'

She was very young, really; certainly far younger than she wanted people to think. For a second she looked like a little girl in a panic. At moments like this she would fix her gaze on the clock, as if seeking inspiration. Her body shook imperceptibly. She must have been very tired. The sergeant picked up a slight whiff of sweat from her armpits mixed with the smell of her perfume.

'What did he say about killing her?' he repeated.

'I can't remember. You know I wasn't on my own. I couldn't listen the whole time.'

'Albert was feeling you up?'

'No. He was holding my hands. The older one said something like: "I've decided to finish it tonight."'

'That doesn't mean he's going to kill her. It could mean he's going to steal her jewellery. No reason he couldn't be a creditor who's just decided to send in the bailiffs.'

'No,' she said, with a certain stubbornness.

'How do you know?'

'Because it's not like that.'

'He explicitly talked about killing her?'

'I'm sure that's what he wants to do. I don't remember how he put it exactly.'

'It couldn't be a misunderstanding?'

'No.'

'And this was two hours ago?'

'A bit longer.'

'So, even though you knew a man was going to commit a crime, you waited until now to come and tell us?'

'I was scared. I couldn't leave Picratt's before it shut. Alfonsi is very strict about that.'

'Even if you'd told him the truth?'

'He'd probably have told me to mind my own business.'

'Try to remember everything they said.'

'They didn't talk much. I didn't hear everything. The band was playing. Then Tania did her act.'

The sergeant had been taking notes for a few minutes, but in an offhand way, without much conviction.

'Do you know a countess?'

'I don't think so.'

'Is there one who goes to the club?'

'We don't get many women coming in. I've never heard of a customer who might be a countess.'

'You didn't manage to get a look at the two men's faces?'

'I didn't dare. I was afraid.'

'Afraid of what?'

'That they'd know I'd heard.'

'What did they call each other?'

'I didn't notice. I've a feeling one of them is called Oscar. I'm not sure. I think I've drunk too much. I've got a head-ache. I want to go to bed. If I'd thought you wouldn't believe me, I wouldn't have come here.'

'Take a seat.'

'Aren't I allowed to leave?'

'Not this minute.'

He pointed to a bench against the wall, under the usual black and white administrative notices.

Then he immediately called her back.

'Your name?'

'Arlette.'

'Your real name. Have you got your identity card?'

She took it out of her handbag and passed it to him. He read: 'Jeanne-Marie-Marcelle Leleu, twenty-four years old, born in Moulins, choreographic artist, 42 *ter*, Rue Notre-Dame-de-Lorette, Paris.'

'You're not called Arlette?'

'It's my stage name.'

'Have you done any acting?'

'Not in real theatres.'

He shrugged and, after writing down her particulars, gave her back her card.

'Go and sit down.'

Then he quietly asked his young colleague to keep an eye on her, went into the next-door office, where he could make a telephone call in private, and called the Police Emergency Service.

'Is that you, Louis? Simon here, La Rochefoucauld station. There hasn't been a countess murdered tonight by any chance, has there?'

'Why a countess?'

'I don't know. It's probably a joke. The girl looks a bit crazy. At any rate, she's drunk. Apparently she heard some guys plotting to murder a countess, a countess who supposedly owns some jewellery.'

'Dunno. Nothing on the board.'

'If there's anything like that, let me know.'

They talked a little longer about this and that. When Simon returned to reception, Arlette had fallen asleep, like someone in the waiting room at a railway station. The resemblance was so striking that he automatically looked for a suitcase at her feet.

At seven in the morning, when Jacquart came to relieve Sergeant Simon, she was still asleep, and Simon filled his colleague in. He saw her wake up as he was leaving, but preferred not to hang around.

She gazed in astonishment at the new policeman, who had a black moustache, then anxiously looked round for the clock and jumped up.

'I have to go,' she said.

'One moment, sweetheart.'

'What do you want from me?'

'Maybe your memory is better after a nap than it was last night.'

She looked sullen now, and her skin had become shiny, especially around her plucked eyebrows.

'I don't know anything else. I've got to go home.'

'What was Oscar like?'

'What Oscar?'

The man was looking at the report Simon had written while she was asleep.

'The one who wanted to murder the countess.'

'I didn't say he was called Oscar.'

'What was he called then?'

'I don't know. I can't remember what I said any more. I'd been drinking.'

'So the whole story's untrue?'

'I didn't say that. I heard two men talking in the next booth, but I only caught snatches of what they were saying, the odd word here and there. Maybe I got it wrong.'

'So why did you come here?'

'I've already told you I'd been drinking. When you've been drinking, you see things differently, you make a drama out of everything.'

'There was no mention of the countess?'

'Yes, there was . . . I think . . .'

'Her jewellery?'

'They talked about jewellery.'

'And about finishing her off?'

'That's what I thought I understood. I was drunk by then.'

'Who had you been drinking with?'

13

'Some customers.'

'One of whom was called Albert?'

'Yes. I don't know him either. I only know people by sight.'

'Including Oscar?'

'Why do you keep saying that name?'

'Would you recognize him?'

'I only saw him from behind.'

'A person's back can be very easy to recognize.'

'I'm not sure. Maybe.'

Struck by a sudden thought, it was her turn to ask, 'Has someone been killed?'

When he didn't answer, she became very nervous. She must have had a terrible hangover. The blue of her eyes was washed out, somehow, and her smudged lipstick made her mouth look enormous.

'Can't I go home?'

'Not right now.'

'I haven't done anything.'

There were a number of policemen in the room now, getting on with their work and swapping stories. Jacquart called the Police Emergency Service, who hadn't heard anything about a dead countess yet, then, to cover his back, telephoned Quai des Orfèvres. Lucas, who had just come on duty and wasn't completely awake, replied, just in case:

'Send her over to me.'

After which he didn't give it another thought. Maigret arrived soon after and glanced through the night's reports before taking off his overcoat and hat.

It was still raining. It was a clammy day. Most people were in a bad mood that morning.

A few minutes after nine o'clock, a Ninth Arrondissement policeman brought Arlette to Quai des Orfèvres. He was a new recruit who wasn't familiar with the building yet and knocked on several doors, as the young woman trailed behind.

This was how he came to knock on the door of the inspectors' office, where young Lapointe was smoking a cigarette, perched on the edge of a desk.

'Sergeant Lucas, please?'

He didn't notice Lapointe and Arlette looking at each other intently and when he was directed to the neighbouring office he shut the door again.

'Sit down,' Lucas said to the dancer.

Maigret, who was doing his usual rounds while waiting for the briefing, happened to be in Lucas' office, standing by the fireplace, filling a pipe.

'This girl,' Lucas explained to him, 'claims to have heard two men plotting to murder a countess.'

She was very different to how she had been before: in a clear, almost shrill voice, she replied:

'I never said that.'

'You said you had heard two men . . .'

'I was drunk.'

'So you made it all up?'

'Yes.'

'Why?'

'I don't know. I was feeling blue. I was bored at the thought of going home and sort of went into the police station by accident.'

Maigret gave her a curious glance, then carried on looking through some papers.

'So there's never been a mention of a countess?'

'No.'

'None whatsoever?'

'Maybe I heard someone talking about a countess. You know, sometimes a word jumps out when people are talking, and it sticks in your mind.'

'Last night?'

'Probably.'

'And that's what you based your story on?'

'What, do you always know what you're saying when you've been drinking?'

Maigret smiled. Lucas looked annoyed.

'Don't you know it's a crime?'

'What?'

'To make a false statement. You could be prosecuted for wasting . . .'

'I don't care. All I'm asking is to be able to go to bed.'

'Do you live on your own?'

'Of course!'

Maigret smiled again.

'You've no memory either of the customer who you drank a bottle of champagne with and who held your hands, a man by the name of Albert?'

'I can barely remember anything. Do I have to do you a drawing? Everyone at Picratt's will tell you I was dead drunk.'

'Since when?'

'I'd got started yesterday evening, if you want all the details.'

'Who with?'

'By myself.'

'Where?'

'All over, really. Different bars. You can tell you've never lived on your own.'

It was a funny thing to say about young Lucas, when he was trying so hard to look stern.

Judging from the weather so far, it was going to rain all day, a cold, monotonous rain falling from a low sky, with the lights on in all the offices and damp patches on the floors.

Lucas was dealing with another case, a break-in at a warehouse on Quai de Javel, and he was in a hurry to get going. He looked questioningly at Maigret.

'What do I do with her?' he seemed to ask.

As the bell for the briefing rang at that moment, Maigret just shrugged, as if to say: 'It's your case.'

'Do you have a telephone?' the sergeant asked again.

'There's a telephone in the concierge's lodge.'

'Do you rent a room?'

'No. I have my own apartment.'

'By yourself?'

'I've already said that.'

'You're not scared you'll run into Oscar if I let you go?'

'I want to go home.'

She couldn't be detained indefinitely for making up a story in her local police station.

'Call me if he shows up again,' declared Lucas, getting to his feet. 'I assume you're not planning on leaving town?'

'No. Why?'

He opened the door for her and watched her walk away down the huge corridor, then hesitate at the top of the stairs. Heads turned as she passed. You sensed she came from a different world, the world of the night, and there was something almost indecent about her in the harsh light of a winter's day.

In his office, Lucas inhaled the smell she had left behind her, a woman's smell, almost the smell of bed. He telephoned the Police Emergency Service again.

'No countess?'

'Nothing to report.'

Then he opened the door of the inspectors' office.

'Lapointe . . .' he called without looking.

A voice, not the young inspector's, replied:

'He's just popped out.'

'He didn't say where he was going?'

'He said he'd be back straight away.'

'Tell him I need him. Not about Arlette or the countess, but to come to Javel with me.'

Lapointe returned a quarter of an hour later. The two men put on their coats and hats and went and caught the Métro at Châtelet.

When Maigret left the commissioner's office, where the daily briefing had been held, he settled down in front of a stack of files, lit a pipe and promised himself not to stir all morning.

It must have been around 9.30 when Arlette left the Police Judiciaire. No one spared a thought as to whether she had taken the Métro or bus to get to Rue Notre-Dame-de-Lorette.

Maybe she stopped at a bar to eat a croissant and drink a café-crème?

The concierge didn't see her get back. It was a busy building, it's true, just round the corner from Place Saint-Georges.

Eleven o'clock was just about to strike when the concierge set about sweeping Building B's stairs and was surprised to see Arlette's door ajar.

At Javel, meanwhile, Lapointe was distracted and preoccupied. Thinking he looked strange, Lucas asked him if he didn't feel well.

'I think I'm coming down with a cold.'

The two men were still questioning the neighbours of the burgled warehouse when the telephone rang in Maigret's office.

'This is the detective chief inspector, Saint-Georges district.'

It was the station on Rue de La Rochefoucauld, which Arlette had gone into at about 4.30 that morning and ended up falling asleep on a bench.

'My secretary tells me we sent over to you this morning a girl called Jeanne Leleu, known as Arlette, who claimed to have overheard a conversation about the murder of a countess.'

'I think I know who you mean,' replied Maigret, frowning. 'Is she dead?'

'Yes. She's just been found strangled in her bedroom.'

'Was she in bed?'

'No.'

'Dressed?'

'Yes.'

'In her coat?'

'No. She was wearing a black silk dress. At least that's what my men told me a minute ago. I haven't gone over there yet. I wanted to telephone you first. It seems that there was something in it after all.'

'It certainly does.'

'Still no news of the countess?'

'Nothing so far. It may take a while.'

'Are you going to see that the prosecutor's informed?'

'I'll telephone now, then head over.'

'I think that would be better. Strange business, isn't it? My night sergeant wasn't too concerned because she was drunk. See you in a moment.'

'See you then.'

Maigret wanted to take Lucas with him but, finding his office empty, he remembered the Javel business. Lapointe wasn't around either. Janvier had just got back and was still wearing his cold, wet raincoat.

'Come on!'

He crammed two pipes in his pocket, as always.

2.

Janvier pulled the Police Judiciare's little car over to the kerb, and both men craned forwards simultaneously in their seats to check the number of the building, then looked at one another in surprise. There was no throng of people on the pavement, or under the arch, or in the courtyard, and the police officer, whom the local station had sent out of habit to keep order, was idly pacing up and down a little way off.

They would soon discover the reason for this aberration. The local detective chief inspector, Monsieur Beulant, opened the door of the lodge to greet them, and at his side stood the concierge, a tall, calm, intelligent-looking woman.

'Madame Boué,' he said, by way of introduction. 'She is married to one of our sergeants. When she discovered the body, she locked the door with her master key and came down to telephone me. No one in the building knows yet.'

She inclined her head slightly, as if being given a compliment.

'Isn't there anyone up there?' asked Maigret.

'Inspector Lognon went up with the doctor from Public Records. In the meantime I've been having a long conversation with Madame Boué, and we have both been trying to work out who this countess might be.'

'I can't think of any countess round here,' she said.

It was clear from her manner and the way she talked that she was intent on being a model witness.

'There was no harm in that girl. We didn't have many dealings, because she used to come home in the early hours and sleep most of the day.'

'Had she been living in the block for long?'

'Two years. She had a two-room apartment in Building B at the end of the courtyard.'

'Did she have many visitors?'

'None, really.'

'Any men?'

'If there were, I didn't see them. Except at the start. When she moved in and her furniture arrived, once or twice I saw an older man who I thought was her father for a moment, a short fellow with very broad shoulders. He never spoke to me. As far as I know, he hasn't been back since. A lot of the building is rented, especially the offices in Building A, and there's always people coming and going.'

'I'll probably be back for a chat soon.'

The building was old. Under the archway a staircase led off to the left and another to the right, both of them dark, with plaques in imitation marble or enamel on the walls advertising a ladies' hairdressers on the mezzanine, a masseuse on the second floor, and on the third, an artificial flower business, a law firm and even an extra-lucid clairvoyant. The courtyard's cobbles glistened with rain, and the door facing them had a black 'B' painted above it.

They went up three floors, leaving dark footprints on the stairs. Only one of the doors opened as they passed, that of a stout woman with thinning hair in curlers, who looked at them with astonishment, then shut her door and locked it.

Inspector Lognon from the Saint-Georges station greeted them, as lugubrious as ever, and gave Maigret a look as if to say: 'I knew it!'

What he knew wasn't that the young woman would be strangled but that, the minute a crime was committed in his neighbourhood and Lognon sent to the scene, Maigret would immediately arrive in person and take the case out of his hands.

'I haven't touched anything,' he said in his most official manner. 'The doctor is still in the bedroom.'

No apartment would have looked cheerful in that weather. It was one of those bleak days when you wonder what you're on earth for in the first place and why you're going to so much trouble to stay here.

The first room was a sitting room of a sort, nicely furnished, meticulously clean and, unexpectedly, as neat as a pin. Maigret was immediately struck by the floor, which was waxed as carefully as in a convent and gave off a pleasant smell of floor polish. He made a note to ask the concierge later if Arlette did the housework herself.

Through the half-open door, Doctor Pasquier could be seen putting his overcoat back on and replacing his instruments in his bag. On the white goatskin rug at the foot of the untouched bed, a body was stretched out: black satin dress, chalk white arm, auburn hair.

What is most moving is always an absurd detail and, in this case, what caused Maigret a momentary stab of anguish was, next to a foot still in its high heel, a foot out of its shoe, the toes visible through a silk stocking which was covered with flecks of mud and had a ladder starting at the heel and going up over the knee.

'Dead, obviously,' said the doctor. 'The guy who did it didn't let go until the end.'

'Can you work out when it happened?'

'Barely an hour and a half ago. Rigor mortis hasn't set in yet.'

Near the bed, behind the door, Maigret had noticed an open wardrobe full of dresses, particularly evening dresses, mainly black.

'You think she was grabbed from behind?'

'Probably, because I don't see any signs of a struggle. Do I send my report to you, Monsieur Maigret?'

'If you don't mind.'

The pretty bedroom wasn't what you would expect of a cabaret dancer's. As in the sitting room, everything was in its place except for the faux mink coat tossed on the bed and the handbag on an armchair.

Maigret explained:

'She left Quai des Orfèvres around nine thirty. If she took a taxi, she got here around ten o'clock. If she came by Métro or bus, she probably got back a little later. She was attacked immediately.'

He went over to the wardrobe, inspected the bottom.

'Someone was waiting for her. Someone was hidden here, who grabbed her by the throat as soon as she took off her coat.'

It had only just happened. It was rare for them to have a chance to be on a crime scene so quickly.

'You don't need me any more, do you?' asked the doctor.

He took his leave. The local police chief also asked if he needed to stay until the public prosecutor got there and wasted no time getting back to his office, which was minutes away. As for Lognon, he was expecting to be told he wasn't needed either and was standing in a corner with a sullen expression.

'Have you found anything?' Maigret asked him, filling his pipe.

'I glanced in the drawers. Look at the left-hand one in the chest of drawers.'

It was full of photographs, all of Arlette. Some were publicity shots like the ones outside Picratt's. They showed her in a black silk dress, not the day dress that was on her body now, but a very tight-fitting evening dress.

'You're a local, Lognon. Did you see her act?'

'I didn't, but I know what it involved. As far as dancing went, as you can tell from the photos on top there, she wiggled about more or less in time with the music while slowly taking off her dress. She didn't wear anything underneath. By the end of the act she was as naked as the day she was born.'

Lognon's long, bulbous nose seemed to be twitching and going red.

'Apparently it's what they do in America in the burlesques. When she was wearing nothing at all, the lights went out.'

He hesitated, then added, 'You should look under her dress.'

While Maigret stalled, surprised, he explained, 'The doctor who examined her called me to show me. She is completely shaved. Even in the street she didn't wear anything underneath.'

Why were all three of them embarrassed? Without a word, they avoided looking at the body lying on the goat-skin rug, which still had something vaguely lascivious about it. Maigret merely glanced at the other photographs, which were in a smaller format, probably taken with an ordinary camera, and showed the young woman, naked throughout, in sexual poses.

'Try to find me an envelope,' he said.

That idiot Lognon sniggered silently at this, as if he were accusing Maigret of taking the photos so he could titillate himself at his leisure in his office.

Next door Janvier had begun a meticulous inspection of the apartment: everywhere showed the same mismatch between what met the eye and these photographs, between Arlette's home and her professional life.

In a cupboard, they found a paraffin stove, two very clean saucepans and a selection of plates, cups and cutlery, indicating that she did at least some of her cooking. Hanging from the window over the courtyard, a meat-safe contained eggs, butter, some celery and two cutlets.

Another cupboard was crammed with brooms, cloths and tins of floor polish, all of which suggested an orderly existence, a housekeeper proud of her home, if not a shade over-zealous.

They looked for letters or papers, without success. A few magazines were lying about, but no books, other than a cookbook and a dictionary. None of those photographs of parents, friends or lovers that you find in most homes either.

There were lots of pairs of shoes with exaggeratedly high heels, the majority virtually brand new, as if Arlette were crazy about shoes or had sensitive feet and found it difficult to get the right fit.

In the handbag, a compact, some keys, a lipstick, an identity card and a handkerchief without initials. Maigret put the identity card in his pocket. Feeling ill at ease in those two cramped rooms, with the radiators blasting out heat, he turned to Janvier.

'You wait for the prosecutor. I'll meet you back here, probably, in a while. Criminal Records won't be long.'

Unable to find an envelope, he stuffed the photos in his overcoat pocket, smiled at Lognon, whom his colleagues had already nicknamed Inspector Hard-done-by, and hurried off down the stairs.

They were going to have to work their way slowly and meticulously through the block, question all the tenants, including the stout woman with the curlers who looked as if she took an interest in what happened on the stairs and may have seen the murderer going up or coming down.

Maigret stopped at the lodge first and asked Madame Boué if he could use the telephone, which was near the bed, under a photograph of Monsieur Boué in uniform.

'Is Lucas back?' he asked, once he was through to the Police Judiciaire. He dictated the particulars on the identity card to another inspector.

'Get in touch with Moulins. Try to find out if she still has family. We need to find anyone who knew her. If her parents are still alive, see they're informed. I assume they'll come immediately.'

He was walking away along the pavement, heading up towards Rue Pigalle, when he heard a car pull up. It was the public prosecutor. Criminal Records would be close behind, and he preferred not to be there, any moment now, when twenty people would be bustling about those two little rooms where the body was still lying in the same position.

There was a bakery on the left and, on the right, a wine seller with a yellow shop front. No doubt Picratt's made more impact at night thanks to its neon sign, standing out against the darkened buildings on either side, but in the day, you could have walked past it without suspecting a nightclub even existed.

The façade was narrow, just a door and a window, and, in the rain and murky light, its display of photographs looked seedy and depressing.

It was after midday. Maigret was surprised to find the door open. An electric light was on inside, and a woman was sweeping between the tables.

'Is the owner here?' he asked.

She looked at him unconcerned, broom in hand, and asked, 'Why?'

'I'd like to talk to him in person . . .'

'He's asleep. I'm his wife.'

She was in her fifties, maybe getting on for sixty. She was fat, but vivacious with it, with beautiful brown eyes in a puffy face.

'Detective Chief Inspector Maigret, of the Police Judiciaire.'

Still no sign of her being flustered.

'Do you want to sit down?'

It was dark inside, and the red of the walls and the curtains looked almost black. Only the bottles behind the bar, near the still open door, reflected the odd glint of daylight.

The room was long and narrow and low-ceilinged, with a cramped stage for the musicians containing a piano and an accordion in its case. Around the dance-floor, there was a set of booths formed by partitions roughly one and a half metres high, which afforded the customers a measure of privacy.

'Do I need to wake Fred up?'

She was in slippers, with a grey apron over an old dress, and hadn't washed or done her hair yet.

'Are you here at night?'

She said simply:

'I keep an eye on the lavatories and do the cooking if customers want to eat.'

'You live here?'

'On the mezzanine. There's a staircase at the back that runs from the kitchen up to our flat. But we've got a house in Bougival, where we go when the place is closed.'

He didn't get the impression she was worried. Intrigued, certainly, to see such an important member of the police calling on her establishment, but otherwise it was nothing new, and she was waiting patiently.

'Have you had this club for long?'

'It'll be eleven years next month.'

'Do you get a lot of customers?'

'Depends what day it is.'

He saw a little printed card on which was written in English:

> Finish the night at Picratt's,
> The hottest spot in Paris.

The little English he remembered allowed him to translate:

> Finissez la nuit au Picratt's,
> L'endroit le plus excitant de Paris.

Excitant wasn't right. The English word was more expressive. *L'endroit le plus chaud de Paris*, that was better, with a very specific sense of *chaud*.

She was still looking at him calmly.

'Do you want anything to drink?'

She knew he would refuse.

'Where do you hand out these flyers?'

'We give them to the doormen of the big hotels, who slip them to their guests, especially the Americans. At night, late at night, when the foreigners are starting to get bored of the big clubs and have run out of places to go, the Grasshopper prowls around, thrusting cards into people's hands and dropping them in cars and taxis. Basically we start working pretty much when the others stop. Get it?'

He got it. More often than not the people who came here would have trailed all over Montmartre without finding what they were looking for, and this was their last shot.

'Most of your customers must be half-drunk when they get here?'

'Of course.'

'Did you have a lot of people last night?'

'It was Monday. We never get a crowd on Mondays.'

'From where you sit, can you see everything that goes on in the club?'

She pointed to a door marked 'W.C.' at the end of the room, on the left of the stage. There was a matching door without a sign on the right.

'I'm almost always over there. We're not that keen on serving food, but sometimes customers will ask for some onion soup, or foie gras, or cold lobster. Then I'll pop into the kitchen for a moment.'

'Otherwise you stay in here?'

'Mostly. I keep an eye on the girls and at the right moment I come over with a box of chocolates or some flowers or a satin doll. You know how it works, right?'

She wasn't trying to sugar the pill. She had sat down with a sigh of relief and taken one foot out of her slippers, a swollen, misshapen foot.

'What's this all about? I don't want to rush you, but it will soon be time to go and wake Fred up. He's a man and he needs more sleep than me.'

'What time did you go to bed?'

'Around five. Sometimes I don't turn in before seven.'

'And when did you get up?'

'An hour ago. I've had time to sweep up, you see.'

'Your husband went to bed at the same time as you?'

'He went up five minutes before me.'

'He didn't go out this morning?'

'He hasn't got out of bed.'

She was becoming a little worried by all this talk of her husband.

'This isn't to do with him, is it?'

'Not especially. It's about two men who came here last night, around two in the morning, and sat in one of the booths. Do you remember that?'

'Two men?'

She looked round the tables, as though thinking back.

'Do you remember where Arlette was sitting before she did her act for the second time?'

'She was with her young man, that's right. I even told her she was wasting her time.'

'Does he come often?'

'He's been three or four times recently. You get ones like that who end up here by mistake and fall in love with one of the women. As I always say to them, you can go there once if you fancy, but make sure they don't come back. The pair of them were over there, in the third booth from the door, number six. I could see them from where I am. He spent the whole time holding her hands and telling her stories with that moony look they always get.'

'What about in the next booth?'

'I didn't see anyone.'

'Not at any point in the evening?'

'We can easily find out. The tables haven't been wiped down yet. If there were any customers at that one, it should still have damp rings from their glasses and cigarette or cigar butts in the ashtray.'

She didn't move while he went to check for himself.

'I can't see anything.'

'Any other day I would be less certain, but Mondays are so dead we've thought of not even opening. I'd swear we didn't get a dozen customers all night. My husband will be able to confirm it.'

'Do you know Oscar?' he asked point-blank.

She didn't start but he had the feeling she became a little more guarded.

'Which Oscar?'

'An older man, short, burly, grey hair.'

'Doesn't ring a bell. The butcher is called Oscar, but he's tall and brown-haired with a moustache. Perhaps my husband . . . ?'

'Go and fetch him, will you?'

He was left sitting on his own in what felt like a purple tunnel, with the door on to the street at the end, a pale grey rectangle that looked like a screen criss-crossed by the flickering figures of an old newsreel.

On the wall facing him, he saw a photograph of Arlette in the inevitable black dress, which clung so tightly to her body that she looked more naked in it than in the obscene photographs he had in his pocket.

He had hardly taken any notice of her this morning, in Lucas' office. She was just another little creature of the night, like so many others. He had been struck by how young she was, though, and something had seemed wrong. He could still hear her tired voice, the voice they all get early in the morning after they have drunk and smoked too much. He pictured her worried eyes, remembered a glance he had automatically darted at her breasts, and, most of all, the woman's smell she had given off, almost the smell of a warm bed.

He had rarely come across a woman who gave such a strong impression of sexuality, and it jarred with the anxious little girl's look in her eyes, and even more with the apartment he had just visited, the beautifully polished floor, the broom cupboard, the meat-safe.

'Fred's coming right down.'

'Did you ask him?'

'I asked him if he'd noticed two men. He doesn't remember them. In fact, he's sure there weren't two customers sitting at that table. Number four. We use numbers for the tables. There was definitely an American at five, who drank a bottle of whisky, and a large group, including some women, at eleven. Désiré, the waiter, will be able to back me up tonight.'

'Where does he live?'

'In the suburbs. I don't know exactly where. He gets a train home from Gare Saint-Lazare in the morning.'

'Do you have other staff?'

'The Grasshopper, who opens car doors, carries bags and hands out flyers now and then. And the musicians and the women.'

'How many women?'

'Apart from Arlette, there's Betty Bruce. Her photo's on the left there, you see. She does acrobatic dances. And then Tania, who is on the piano when she's not doing her turn. That's all for the moment. Obviously there are girls who come in to have a drink, hoping to meet someone, but they're not part of the family. This is a family business here. We're not ambitious, Fred and me, and when we've put enough money aside, we're going to live a quiet life in our house in Bougival. Look, here he is . . .'

A man in his fifties, short and powerfully built, in a perfect state of preservation, his hair still black apart from a few flecks of silver at the temples, came out of the kitchen, putting on a jacket over his collarless shirt. He must have grabbed the first clothes he could find because he was wearing evening trousers and slippers without socks.

He was calm too, even calmer than his wife, in fact. He would have known Maigret's name, though this was the first time he had been in his presence, and he took his time coming over so he could size him up.

'Fred Alfonsi,' he introduced himself, holding out his hand. 'My wife hasn't given you anything to drink?'

He ran the palm of his hand over table four, as if setting his mind at rest about something.

'You really don't want anything? You won't mind if Rose goes and makes me a cup of coffee?'

His wife headed towards the kitchen and disappeared through the door. The man sat down opposite Maigret, his elbows on the table, and waited.

'You're sure there were no customers at this table last night?'

'Listen, inspector. I know who you are, but you don't know me, do you? Maybe you had a word with your colleagues from the Vice Squad before you came. Those gentlemen drop in from time to time to see me. It's their job, and they've been doing it for years. If they haven't done so already, they'll tell you I'm harmless.'

As he said this, Maigret was amused to notice his ex-boxer's flattened nose and cauliflower ears.

'If I tell you there wasn't anyone at that table, that's because there wasn't. This is a modest establishment I've got here. There's only a few of us running the show, and I always keep an eye on everything. I could tell you exactly how many people we had in last night. I'd just have to check the dockets for each table at the till.'

'So Arlette was definitely at five with her young man?'

'She was at six. The even numbers are on the right: two, four, six, eight, ten, twelve. The odd are on the left.'

'And at the next table?'

'Eight? There were two couples, at about four in the morning. Parisians, who'd never been here before, hadn't known where to go and soon realized that it wasn't their kind of thing. They just had a bottle of champagne, then left. I closed up almost immediately after that.'

'So you didn't see two men sitting on their own, either at that table or at any other one, one of whom was middle-aged, answering more or less to your description?'

Fred Alfonsi smiled as if he'd heard it all before, then replied:

'If you stop trying to trap me, maybe I could be of some use to you. Don't you think we've had enough cat and mouse?'

'Arlette's dead.'

'What?' he exclaimed with a start.

Shaken, he got to his feet, shouted towards the back of the club, 'Rose! Rose!'

'Yes . . . I'll be right there . . .'

'Arlette's dead!'

'What are you saying?'

She hurried over surprisingly fast, given her size.

'Arlette?' she repeated.

'She was strangled this morning in her bedroom,' Maigret went on, looking at both of them.

'Oh my God! Who's the bastard who . . .'

'That's what I'm trying to find out.'

Rose blew her nose, and he could feel she was on the verge of tears. Her eyes were fixed on the photograph hanging on the wall.

'How did it happen?' asked Fred, heading towards the bar.

He carefully chose a bottle, filled three glasses and went and gave one to his wife first. It was an old liqueur brandy, and, without pressing the point, he put a glass in front of Maigret, who ended up taking a sip.

'She overheard a conversation here, last night, between two men about a countess.'

'What countess?'

'I've no idea. She thought one of the two men was called Oscar.'

No reaction.

'When she left here, she went to the local station to report what she'd heard, and they took her to Quai des Orfèvres.'

'Is that why she was done in?'

'Probably.'

'Did you see two men together, Rose?'

She said she hadn't. Each of them looked as genuinely shocked and heartbroken as the other.

'I swear that if two men had been in here I would know and I would tell you. There's no need for us to play games. You know how a club like this works. People don't come here to see great acts, or dance to the finest jazz. Or for the elegant surroundings. You've read the flyer. They go to other clubs first on the hunt for some excitement. If they pick up a girl, we don't see them. But, if they haven't found what they fancy, they end up at our place, more often than not, and by then they're pie-eyed. Most of the cab drivers who work nights are hand in glove with me, and I tip them well. Some of the doormen of the big clubs have a word in their clientele's ears as they're leaving. Mostly we get foreigners, who think they're going to find something extraordinary. Well, the only thing that was extraordinary was Arlette, who took her clothes off. For a quarter of a second, when her dress was on the floor, they saw her completely naked. To avoid trouble, I asked her to shave herself, because apparently it looks less rude. Afterwards, it was rare someone didn't invite her over to his table.'

'Did she sleep with them?' Maigret asked carefully.

'Not here, at any rate. And not during working hours. I don't let the girls leave the building when we're open. They keep men here as long as they can by getting them to drink, and I suppose they promise to meet up with them when they get off.'

'Do they?'

'What do you think?'

'Arlette as well?'

'She must have.'

'With the young man from last night?'

'Not in a million years. He had what you'd call good intentions. He happened to come in one night with a friend and he fell in love with Arlette on the spot. He came back a few times, but he'd never stay until closing time. Probably had to get up early to go to work.'

'Did she have other regulars?'

'There are hardly any regulars in this place, you must have worked that out. Everyone's just passing through. They're all the same, of course, but they're always new.'

'Did she have any friends?'

'No idea,' he said, rather coldly.

Maigret looked hesitantly at Fred's wife.

'You never . . .'

'You can ask. Rose isn't jealous; it hasn't bothered her for years. I did, yes, if you must know . . .'

'At her place?'

'I've never set foot in her place. Here. In the kitchen.'

'That's always his way,' said Rose. 'There's barely time to notice he's gone and he's back already. Then the girl comes out, ruffling her feathers like a chicken.'

That made her laugh.

'Do you know anything about the countess?'

'What countess?'

'Doesn't matter. Can you give me the Grasshopper's address? What's his real name?'

'Thomas . . . He has no surname . . . He was brought up in care. I can't tell you where he rests his head, but you'll find him at the races this afternoon. That's the only thing he cares about. Another one?'

'No, thank you.'

'Do you think journalists are going to show up?'

'I daresay. When they find out.'

It was difficult to tell if Fred was delighted or annoyed by the publicity this would bring him.

'Either way, I'm here if you need me. I suppose it's better if I open as usual tonight. If you want to drop by, you can question everyone.'

When Maigret got to Rue Notre-Dame-de-Lorette, the prosecutor's car had gone and an ambulance was driving off with the young woman's body. There was a little group of gawkers at the door, but fewer than one might have imagined. He found Janvier in the concierge's lodge, talking on the telephone. When the inspector hung up, he reported:

'We've already had word from Moulins. The Leleus are both still alive, father and mother, and there's a son who works in a bank. As for Jeanne Leleu, the daughter, she's a little brunette with a flat nose who left home three years ago and hasn't sent word since. The parents don't want to hear her name ever again.'

'The description doesn't fit at all?'

'Not at all. She is five centimetres shorter than Arlette and is unlikely to have had her nose straightened.'

'No calls about the countess?'

'Nothing on that. I've questioned the tenants of B. There's a lot of them. The big blonde who watched us going up checks coats at a theatre. She claims not to take any notice of what goes in the building, but she did hear someone go past a few minutes before the girl.'

'So she heard her go up? How did she recognize it was her?'

'By her walk, she says. In fact her door's open a crack the whole time.'

'Did she see the man?'

'She says she didn't, but that he climbed the stairs slowly, like someone who was heavyset or a man suffering from a bad heart.'

'She didn't hear him come back down?'

'No.'

'She's sure it wasn't a tenant from the upper floors?'

'She recognizes all the tenants by their tread. I saw Arlette's neighbour as well, a waitress. I had to wake her up, but she hadn't heard anything.'

'Is that it?'

'Lucas rang to say he's back at the office, awaiting orders.'

'Fingerprints?'

'We only lifted ours and Arlette's. You'll have the report this evening.'

'Do you have a tenant called Oscar?' Maigret asked the concierge on the off-chance.

'No, detective chief inspector. But once, a very long time ago, I took a telephone message for Arlette. A man's voice, with a sort of country accent, said: "Will you tell her Oscar is waiting for her? She'll know where."'

'How long ago, roughly, was that?'

'It was a month or two after she had moved in. It struck me because it's the only message I took for her.'

'Did she get post?'

'Letters from Brussels now and then.'

'In a man's hand?'

'A woman's. It wasn't an educated person's handwriting either.'

Half an hour later, Maigret and Janvier, who had had a quick glass of beer at the Brasserie Dauphine, were climbing the stairs at Quai des Orfèvres.

Maigret had barely opened the door of his office when young Lapointe burst in, red-eyed, a frenzied look on his face.

'I've got to talk to you right away, chief.'

When Maigret stepped away from the wardrobe where he had hung up his hat and overcoat, he saw that Lapointe was biting his lips and clenching his fists to stop himself bursting into tears.

3.

Turning away from Maigret, his face almost pressed against the window, Lapointe mumbled:

'When I saw her here this morning, I wondered why she'd been brought in. On our way to Javel, Sergeant Lucas told me what happened. And now, when I get back to the office, I find out she's dead.'

Maigret, who had sat down, said slowly, 'I'd forgotten you're called Albert.'

'After what she'd told him, Monsieur Lucas shouldn't have let her go off by herself, without anybody watching her at all.'

He spoke in the voice of a sulky child, and Maigret smiled.

'Come over here and sit down.'

Lapointe hesitated, as if he was angry with Maigret too. Then, grudgingly, he came and sat down in the chair facing the desk. He still didn't raise his head, staring fixedly at the floor, and, with Maigret gravely taking little draws on his pipe, they looked a bit like a father and son in solemn conversation.

'You haven't been part of the force for very long, but you should know by now that if we had to put everyone who informs on a person under surveillance, you'd never have time to sleep or even grab a sandwich, would you?'

'Yes, chief. But . . .'

'But what?'

'It wasn't the same with her.'

'Why?'

'You can see it wasn't just finger-pointing.'

'Let's hear it, now you're calmer . . .'

'Hear what?'

'Everything.'

'How I met her?'

'If you like. Start at the beginning.'

'I was with a friend from Meulan, a schoolmate, who doesn't get the chance to come to Paris much. We went out with my sister first, then we saw her home, and the two of us went to Montmartre. You know how it is. We had a drink in a couple of clubs and when we came out of the last one, a sort of gnome slipped a flyer into our hands.'

'Why do you say a sort of gnome?'

'Because he looks fourteen but his face is covered with tiny wrinkles, like a worn-out old man. He's the build and height of a street urchin, I suppose that's why they call him the Grasshopper. My friend had been disappointed by the other cabarets, so I thought Picratt's would have something racier on offer, and we went in.'

'How long ago was this?'

He thought back and seemed amazed and saddened somehow by the result. He had no choice but to reply:

'Three weeks.'

'You met Arlette?'

'She came and sat down at our table. My friend, who doesn't know how it all works, thought she was a tart. We had an argument as we left.'

'About her?'

'Yes. I'd already realized she wasn't like the rest.'

Maigret listened without smiling, meticulously cleaning one of his pipes.

'You went back the following night?'

'I wanted to apologize for the way my friend had spoken to her.'

'What did he say to her exactly?'

'He offered her money to sleep with him.'

'She refused?'

'Of course. I went early to be sure there'd be hardly anyone there, and she agreed to have a drink with me.'

'A drink or a bottle?'

'A bottle. The boss doesn't let them sit at a table with customers if you only buy them a drink. And you've got to have champagne.'

'I understand.'

'I know what you're thinking. Still, she came here to tell us what she knew and now she's been strangled.'

'Did she talk of being in any danger?'

'Not exactly. But I knew there were mysterious things in her life.'

'What, for instance?'

'It's difficult to explain, and no one will believe me, because I loved her.'

He said this in an even lower voice, raising his head and looking Maigret in the eye, ready to lash out at any hint of irony.

'I wanted to offer her a new life.'

'Marry her?'

Lapointe hesitated, embarrassed.

'I didn't think of that. I probably wouldn't have married her straight away.'

'But you didn't want her to appear naked in a cabaret any more?'

'I was sure it was making her suffer.'

'She said it was?'

'It's more complicated than that, chief. I realize you'd see the set-up differently. I'm the same, I know the kind of women you meet in those places.

'For a start it was very difficult to know exactly what she was thinking, because she drank. Normally they don't – I'm sure you'd say the same. They pretend to, to get people drinking, but they're given a little glass of some kind of syrup that's meant to look like a liqueur. Isn't that true?'

'Almost always.'

'Arlette drank because she needed to drink. Almost every evening. To the point where, before she did her act, the owner, Monsieur Fred, had to come and check she could stand up.'

Lapointe had become such a part of Picratt's in his mind that he said 'Monsieur Fred', probably as the staff did.

'You never stayed until the morning?'

'She didn't want me to.'

'Why?'

'Because I'd told her that I had to get up early for work.'

'Did you also tell her that you were in the police?'

He blushed again.

'No. I did tell her about my sister though, who I live with, and she used to order me to go home. I never gave her any money. She wouldn't have accepted it. She'd only allow me to buy one bottle, never any more, and always chose the cheapest champagne.'

'You think she was in love?'

'Last night I was sure she was.'

'Why? What did you talk about?'

'Always the same thing, her and me.'

'Did she tell you about herself, what her family did?'

'She made no bones of the fact that she had a fake identity card and that it would be very bad if anyone found out her real name.'

'Was she cultured?'

'I don't know. She definitely wasn't born for that trade. She didn't tell me about her life. She only said that there was a man who she would never be able to get rid of and that it was her fault, that it was too late, that I shouldn't come and see her any more, there was no point, it just hurt her. That's why I say she was falling in love with me. Her hands were clasped in mine as she talked.'

'Was she drunk by then?'

'Maybe. She had definitely been drinking, but she was thinking perfectly clearly. I almost always saw her like

47

that: tense, with a look in her eyes that was either sad or over-excited.'

'Did you sleep with her?'

There was almost hatred in the look he shot Maigret.

'No!'

'You didn't ask her to?'

'No.'

'She didn't offer either?'

'Never.'

'Did she make you think she was a virgin?'

'She'd had to go along with men. She hated them.'

'Why?'

'Because.'

'Because of what?'

'Because of what they had done to her. It was when she was very young, I don't know the details, but it scarred her. She was haunted by a memory. She always talked to me about a man she was very scared of.'

'Oscar?'

'She didn't say his name. You're convinced that she was making fun of me and that I'm naive, aren't you? I don't care. She is dead, and that proves at least that she was right to be scared.'

'You never wanted to sleep with her?'

'The first night I did,' he admitted, 'when I was with my friend. Did you see her when she was alive? Oh yes, just for a few minutes, this morning, when she was exhausted. If you'd seen her under different circumstances, you'd understand . . . Other women don't . . .'

'They don't . . . ?'

'It's too hard to put into words. Everyone was attracted to her. When she did her act . . .'

'Did she sleep with Fred?'

'She had to submit to him, like the others.'

Maigret tried to find out how open Arlette had been.

'Where?'

'In the kitchen. Rose knew. She didn't dare say anything because she is very scared of losing her husband. Have you met her?'

Maigret nodded.

'Did she tell you how old she is?'

'She's in her fifties, I guess.'

'She's nearly seventy. Fred's twenty years younger than her. Apparently she was one of the most beautiful women of her generation and used to be kept by a string of very wealthy men. She really loves him. She doesn't dare show any jealousy and tries to make sure it happens in the club. She thinks it's less risky, you understand?'

'I understand.'

'Arlette scared her more than the others, and she was always watching her. But in a way it was Arlette who made the club work. Without her, no one will go any more. The others are the sort of nice girls you find in every cabaret in Montmartre.'

'What happened last night?'

'Did she talk about it?'

'She told Lucas that you were with her, but she only mentioned your first name.'

'I stayed until two-thirty.'

'At what table?'

'Six.'

He spoke like a regular, almost as if he worked there.

'Were there are any customers in the next booth?'

'Not at four. A whole gang turned up at eight and made a hell of a racket.'

'So that if there had been someone on four, you wouldn't have noticed?'

'I would. I didn't want anyone to hear what I was saying and I kept getting up to look over the partition.'

'You didn't notice a middle-aged man, short and sturdy, with grey hair, at any of the tables?'

'No.'

'As you were talking to her, did Arlette seem to be listening to any other conversation?'

'I'm sure she wasn't. Why?'

'Do you want to work on the investigation with me?'

He looked at Maigret in surprise, then suddenly, overflowing with gratitude, exclaimed:

'You don't mind, even though . . . ?'

'Listen to me, this is important. When she left Picratt's at four in the morning, Arlette went to the station on Rue de La Rochefoucauld. According to the sergeant who heard her out, she was very worked up by then and staggering a bit. She told him about two men who had sat at table four when she was at six with you, and whose conversation she'd partly overheard.'

'Why did she say that?'

'I've no idea. When we know, we'll probably have got somewhere. There's more. The two men were talking about some countess whom one of them was planning to murder. When they left, according to Arlette, she got a very clear sight, from behind, of a middle-aged man, on the short side, with broad shoulders and grey hair. And, while they were talking, she said she overheard the first name Oscar, which seemed to refer to him.'

'But I think I would have heard . . .'

'I saw Fred and his wife. They also say that table four was empty all night and that no one of that description came in to Picratt's. So, Arlette knew something. She didn't want to, or wasn't able to, admit how she had found it out. She was drunk, you told me. She probably thought we wouldn't check where the customers were sitting. Do you follow me?'

'Yes. How could she come up with a name? Why?'

'Exactly. She wasn't asked. There was no need. If she did it, she must have had a reason. And that reason can only have been to give us a lead. Another thing: at the station, she was emphatic, but once she got here, after she'd had time to sleep off her champagne, she was much more reticent, and Lucas had the feeling she'd happily have retracted everything she'd said. Well, we know now that it wasn't just idle fancy.'

'I'm certain it wasn't.'

'She went home, and someone who was waiting for her, hidden in the wardrobe in her bedroom, strangled her. So it was someone who knew her very well, who was a regular visitor to her apartment and probably had a key.'

'And the countess?'

'No news so far. Either she hasn't been killed or the body hasn't been found, which is possible. She never talked to you about a countess?'

'Never.'

Lapointe sat staring at the desk for a long while, then asked in a different voice:

'Do you think she suffered very much?'

'Not for long. It was done by someone very strong, and she didn't even struggle.'

'Is she still there?'

'They've just taken her to the Forensic Institute.'

'Do I have permission to go and see her?'

'After you've had something to eat.'

'Then what should I do?'

'Go to her place, Rue Notre-Dame-de-Lorette. Ask Janvier for the key. We've already examined the flat, but an insignificant detail may mean something to you, seeing as you knew her.'

'Thank you,' he said fervently, convinced Maigret was giving him this job just to make him happy.

Maigret was careful not to draw his attention to the photographs under a file on his desk, their edges poking out.

An orderly came to tell him that five or six reporters were waiting in the corridor, demanding information. He had them brought in, told them only part of the story, but gave each of them one of the photographs of Arlette in her black silk dress.

'Can you also say,' he instructed them, 'that we would be grateful to a certain Jeanne Leleu, who will be living under another name at present, if she would kindly make herself known to us. She is guaranteed absolute discretion, and we have no desire to complicate her existence.'

*

He ate lunch late, at home, then still had time to go back to Quai des Orfèvres and read the Alfonsi file. Paris was as ghostly in the drizzly, dirty rain as it had been earlier, and people seemed to be scurrying about the streets, as if they thought they might be able to escape from the aquarium.

The file on Picratt's owner may have been bulky but it contained almost nothing of substance. At twenty he had done his military service in the penal units of the Battalions of Light Infantry of Africa because he was living off the earnings of a prostitute on Boulevard Sébastopol at the time and had already been arrested twice for assault and battery.

The file then jumped forwards several years to find him in Marseille, where he was procuring women for a number of brothels in the south. He was twenty-eight. He wasn't a big gun yet but he was already high enough up in the hierarchy of that world not to have to get mixed up in brawls in the bars on the Vieux Port any more.

He hadn't had any convictions at this point, just some pretty serious trouble over a girl who was only seventeen and had been employed in the Paradis in Béziers with false papers.

Another gap. All that was known was that he had left for Panama on an Italian vessel with a cargo of five or six women and had become some kind of a kingpin down there.

At forty he was in Paris, living with Rosalie Dumont, known as Rose, a rapidly fading beauty who ran a massage parlour on Rue des Martyrs. He spent a lot of time at the races and the boxing and was thought to take bets.

He finally married Rose, and together they opened Picratt's, which was just a little neighbourhood bar at first.

Janvier was over at Rue Notre-Dame-de-Lorette as well, although not in the apartment. He was still questioning the neighbours who lived in the building, but also the local shopkeepers and anyone who might have known anything. Meanwhile Lucas was finishing off the Javel burglary case on his own, which was doing nothing for his mood.

It was ten to five and had been dark for a long time when the telephone rang and Maigret finally heard the words:

'Police Emergency Service here.'

'The countess?' he asked.

'A countess, at any rate. I don't know if it's yours. We've just had a call from Rue Victor-Massé. A few minutes ago the concierge discovered that one of her tenants had been killed, probably last night.'

'A countess?'

'The Countess von Farnheim.'

'Shot?'

'Strangled. That's all we've got so far. The local police are on the scene.'

Moments later, Maigret jumped into a taxi that wasted an interminable amount of time crossing the centre of Paris. Passing Rue Notre-Dame-de-Lorette, he spotted Janvier coming out of a greengrocer's, told the driver to stop and called to the inspector:

'Get in! The countess is dead.'

'A real countess?'

'I've no idea. It's just round the corner. It's all happening in this neighbourhood.'

It was less than 500 metres, in fact, from the bar on Rue Pigalle to Arlette's flat, and the bar was roughly the same distance from Rue Victor-Massé.

Unlike that morning, twenty or so onlookers were gathered round a policeman at the door of a well-appointed, sedate-looking building.

'Is the detective chief inspector here?'

'He wasn't in the office. It was Inspector Lognon who . . .'

Poor Lognon, so desperate to distinguish himself! Every time he leaped on a case, it was all but inevitable that he would see Maigret show up and snatch it from his grasp.

The concierge wasn't in her lodge. The stairwell had faux marbled walls and a thick dark red carpet on the stairs, held in place by brass rods. The building smelled slightly musty, as if it was inhabited solely by old people who never opened their windows, and it was strangely silent; no hint of rustling doors as Maigret and Janvier passed. Only on the fourth floor did they hear any noise, and a door opened. They glimpsed the long lugubrious nose of Lognon, who was in conversation with a very short, very fat woman whose hair was pulled into a tight bun on the top of her head.

The room they walked into was dimly lit by a standard lamp with a parchment shade. The atmosphere was much more stifling here than in the rest of the building. Without knowing exactly why, they suddenly felt that they were a very long way from Paris and the world, from the damp air outside, the people walking on the pavements, the taxis blowing their horns, the buses pounding by, their brakes screeching every time they stopped.

It was so hot that Maigret immediately took off his overcoat.

'Where is she?'

'In her bedroom.'

The room was a sort of living room, or at least what had once been a living room, but they were entering a world where things no longer had names. An apartment that was up for auction might look like that, with all its furniture in unexpected places.

Bottles were scattered everywhere, and Maigret noticed that they were all red wine, litres of the sort of cheap red you see workmen drinking from the bottle on building sites as they eat salami. There was salami too, for that matter, not on plates but on greasy paper, and leftover chicken, the bones of which they found on the carpet.

Like everything in the room, the carpet was threadbare and incredibly dirty. A chair was missing a leg, horsehair was sticking out of an armchair, and the parchment lampshade, shiny from use, was bent completely out of shape.

In the bedroom next door, on a bed without sheets which looked as if it hadn't been made for days, a body was stretched out half-naked – exactly half, with the upper part more or less covered by a camisole, and the puffy, greyish flesh from the waist to the feet bare.

Maigret instantly saw the little blue spots on the thighs and knew he was going to find a syringe somewhere. He found two, one with a broken needle, on what had served as a bedside table.

The dead woman looked at least sixty. It was hard to tell. No one had touched her yet. The doctor hadn't arrived. But it was clear that she had been dead for a long time.

As for the mattress she was lying on, there was a fairly long cut in the cloth, and part of the stuffing had been ripped out.

There were bottles and leftovers in here too, and a chamber pot with urine in it right in the middle of the room.

'Did she live on her own?' Maigret asked, turning towards the concierge.

The woman nodded, tight-lipped.

'Did she have many visitors?'

'If she had, she'd probably have cleaned up all this filth, don't you think?'

As if she felt personally criticized, the concierge then added:

'It's the first time I've set foot in this apartment for at least three years.'

'Didn't she let you come in?'

'I didn't want to.'

'She didn't have a maid, a cleaning lady?'

'No one. Just a friend, another mad woman like her, who'd come every now and then.'

'Do you know her?'

'I don't know her name but I sometimes see her around the neighbourhood. She isn't quite as far gone yet. At least not the last time I saw her, which was a while ago.'

'Did you know your tenant was on drugs?'

'I knew she was half-crazy.'

'Were you the concierge here when she rented the apartment?'

'She wouldn't have got it if I had been. We've only been here for three years, my husband and I, and she's been in this flat for a good eight. I've tried everything to get her to leave.'

'Is she really a countess?'

'Apparently. At any rate, she was married to a count, but she can't have amounted to much before that.'

'Did she have money?'

'It looks like it, since she didn't starve to death.'

'Did you see anyone going up to her apartment?'

'When?'

'Last night or this morning.'

'No. Her friend hasn't been. Or the young man.'

'What young man?'

'A short, polite, sickly-looking young man, who used to go up to see her and call her his aunt.'

'You don't know his name either?'

'I didn't have anything to do with her carry-on. It's a quiet place otherwise. On the first floor there are people who are hardly ever in Paris, and on the second there's a retired general. You see what sort of building it is. This woman was so dirty I held my nose when I passed her door.'

'Did she never send for the doctor?'

'Oh, only twice a week. When she was as drunk as a skunk on wine, or who knows what, she would get it into her head that she was dying and telephone her doctor. He knew what she was like and would take his time coming over.'

'A local doctor?'

'Doctor Bloch, who lives three buildings along.'

'Did you ring him when you found the body?'

'No. That was none of my business. I told the police straight away. The inspector came. Then you.'

'Do you want to try Doctor Bloch, Janvier? Tell him to come as quickly as possible.'

Janvier looked for the telephone, which he eventually found in another little room among a slew of old magazines and ripped-up books on the floor.

'Is it easy to get into the building without you knowing?'

'All buildings are the same, aren't they?' the concierge replied tartly. 'I do my job just like anyone else, better than most, in fact, and you won't find a speck of dust on the stairs.'

'Are these the only stairs?'

'There's a backstairs, but almost no one uses it. Anyhow, you have to go past the lodge to get to it.'

'Are you in the whole time?'

'Except when I'm doing my shopping. Concierges still have to eat.'

'What time do you do your shopping?'

'Around half past eight in the morning, straight after the postman's been and I've taken up the letters.'

'Did the countess get a lot of post?'

'Only brochures. Tradesmen would see her name in the telephone directory and be amazed by her title.'

'Do you know Monsieur Oscar?'

'Which Oscar?'

'Any Oscar.'

'There's my son.'

'How old is he?'

'Seventeen. He's a carpenter's apprentice in a workshop on Boulevard Barbès.'

'Does he live with you?'

'Of course!'

Janvier, who had hung up, announced:

'The doctor's at his surgery. He's got two more patients to see and then he'll come straight after that.'

Inspector Lognon was taking care not to touch anything and pretending not to be interested in the concierge's answers.

'Your tenant never received letters on bank stationery?'

'Never.'

'Did she go out often?'

'Sometimes she wouldn't leave her apartment for ten, or even twelve days. I'd actually start wondering if she was dead, because you wouldn't hear a sound. She must have been sprawled out on the bed, all sweaty and filthy. Then she'd get dressed, put on a hat and gloves, and you'd almost have taken her for a lady, except she still had that wild-eyed look of hers.'

'Would she be gone for long?'

'It depended. Sometimes a few minutes, sometimes the whole day. She'd come back with masses of packages. She got wine delivered by the crate. Always cheap red, which she'd buy at the grocer's on Rue Condorcet.'

'The deliveryman would go into her flat?'

'He'd leave the crate at the door. I even had an argument with him once because he refused to use the backstairs, which he thought were too dark. He didn't want to break his neck, he said.'

'How did you know she was dead?'

'I didn't know she was dead.'

'You opened the door, though, didn't you?'

'I didn't have to put myself to any trouble and I shouldn't have.'

'Explain.'

'We're on the fourth floor here. On the fifth there's a disabled old gentleman who I clean for and whose meals I take up. He used to be a tax man. He's lived in the same apartment for years and years, and his wife died six months ago. You may have read about it in the paper: she was knocked down by a bus as she was crossing Place Blanche at ten o'clock in the morning on her way to Rue Lepic market.'

'What time do you do his housework?'

'About ten o'clock in the morning. I sweep the stairs on my way down.'

'Did you sweep them this morning?'

'Why wouldn't I?'

'Before that, do you go up with the post first?'

'Not up to the fifth because the old gentleman doesn't get many letters and is in no rush to read them. The people on the third both go out to work and leave early, around eight thirty, so they pick up their post in the lodge on their way past.'

'Even if you're not there?'

'Even when I'm doing my shopping, yes. I never lock up. I buy what I need in the street and take a quick look in the building now and then. Would you mind if I opened the window?'

Everyone was hot. They had gone back into the first room, except for Janvier, who, as he had done that morning at Rue Notre-Dame-de-Lorette, was riffling through drawers and cupboards.

'So you only take the post up to the second floor?'

'Yes.'

'Around ten o'clock you went up to the fifth floor and you passed this door?'

'I noticed it was open slightly. That surprised me a little, but not that much. Coming back down, I didn't pay it any mind. I had got everything ready for my gentleman and didn't have to go back up until four thirty, because that's when I take him his dinner. When I came back down I saw the door was open again and I automatically called quietly: "Countess!" Because everyone calls her that. She has a difficult name to pronounce, something foreign. It's easier to say countess. There was no answer.'

'Were there any lights on in the flat?'

'Yes. I didn't touch anything. This lamp was on.'

'And the one in the bedroom?'

'And that one, because it is now and I haven't touched it. I don't know why I had a bad feeling. I put my head round the door to call again. Then I reluctantly went in. I am very sensitive to smells. I glanced into the bedroom and I saw her. Then I ran downstairs to call the police. As there was no one else in the building apart from the old gentleman, I went to tell the concierge next door, who is a friend, so I wouldn't be all alone. People asked us what was going on. There were a few of us at the door when the inspector arrived.'

'Thank you. What is your name?'

'Madame Aubain.'

'Thank you, Madame Aubain. You can go back to your lodge. I hear footsteps, it must be the doctor.'

It wasn't Doctor Bloch yet, as a matter of fact, but the Public Records doctor, who had also performed the examination at Arlette's that morning.

Going to the bedroom door, after a handshake for Maigret and a vaguely patronizing wave for Lognon, he couldn't help exclaiming, 'Again!'

The bruises on her throat left no doubt as to how the countess had been killed. The blue spots on her thighs were equally conclusive about the extent of her addiction. He sniffed one of the syringes and shrugged: 'Morphine, obviously.'

'You knew her?'

'Never seen her. But I know some of her kind around here. Ah, looks like someone did this to rob her.'

He pointed to the slash in the mattress and the horsehair sticking out.

'Was she rich?'

'We've no idea,' answered Maigret.

Janvier who had been jiggling the lock of a chest of drawers with the tip of his knife for a while, announced:

'Here's a drawer full of papers.'

Someone young was hurrying up the stairs. It was Doctor Bloch.

Maigret noticed that the Public Records doctor merely gave him a fairly dry nod by way of a greeting and refrained from shaking his hand, as one colleague to another.

4.

Doctor Bloch's skin was pasty, his eyes were too bright, and he had black, greasy hair. He couldn't have stopped to listen to the gawkers in the street, or even to speak to the concierge. Janvier hadn't told him on the telephone that the countess had been murdered, just that she was dead and that the detective chief inspector wanted to talk to him.

After taking the stairs four at a time, he looked around anxiously. Maybe he'd shot up before leaving his surgery? He didn't seem surprised that his colleague wouldn't shake hands and didn't make a thing out of it. He had the attitude of someone who expects trouble.

But the moment he set foot in the bedroom, his relief was palpable. The countess had been strangled. It was nothing to do with him now.

It took him less than thirty seconds to regain his poise, as well as a slightly peevish arrogance.

'Why was I sent for and not another doctor?' he asked first, as though testing the ground.

'Because the concierge told us you were this woman's doctor.'

'I only saw her a few times.'

'What was wrong with her?'

Bloch turned deferentially to his colleague, as if to say they were both equally well informed.

65

'I imagine you've gathered she was a drug addict? When she'd heavily indulged, she suffered fits of depression, as often happens, and she'd send for me in a panic. She was very scared of dying.'

'Had you known her long?'

'I only moved into the neighbourhood three years ago.'

He wasn't much over thirty. Maigret would have sworn that he was a bachelor and that he had become addicted to morphine himself as soon as he had started practising, or perhaps even when he was still at medical school. It was no coincidence that he had chosen to set up in Montmartre, and it wasn't hard to imagine the circles within which he recruited his patients.

A brilliant career did not lie ahead of him, that was obvious. He was another person who wouldn't be around for much longer.

'What do you know about her?'

'Her name and her address, which are on my index cards. And that she had been taking drugs for fifteen years.'

'How old is she?'

'Forty-eight or forty-nine.'

Looking at the emaciated body stretched across the bed, the scraggly, colourless hair, it was hard to believe.

'Isn't it pretty unusual for a morphine addict to be hooked on drink too?'

'It happens.'

His hands trembled slightly, like an alcoholic's in the morning, and now and then a twitch dragged down one side of his mouth.

'I suppose you tried to wean her off?'

'In the beginning, yes. She was an all but hopeless case. I didn't get anywhere. She wouldn't speak to me for weeks.'

'Didn't she ever call you because she had run out of drugs and needed some no matter what?'

Bloch glanced at his colleague. There was no point lying. The body and the apartment couldn't have spelled it out more clearly.

'I suppose I don't need to give you a lecture. After a certain point, a drug addict absolutely cannot be deprived of the drug in question without running a serious risk. I don't know where she procured hers. I didn't ask. Twice, I think, when I got here, I found her pretty much out of her mind because a delivery she had been expecting hadn't arrived, and I gave her an injection.'

'She never said anything to you about her life or family or background?'

'All I know is that she really was married to a Count von Farnheim, who I think was Austrian and much older than her. She lived with him on the Côte d'Azur on a large estate which she would sometimes mention.'

'One more question, doctor: did she settle your bills by cheque?'

'No. In cash.'

'I suppose you don't know anything about her friends or relations or suppliers?'

'Nothing whatsoever.'

Maigret didn't insist.

'Thank you. You can go.'

Once again he didn't want to be there when the public prosecutor arrived, let alone answer the reporters who would come running at any moment. He was impatient to get away from that suffocating, depressing atmosphere.

He gave Janvier some instructions, then got a ride to Quai des Orfèvres where a message was waiting for him from Doctor Paul, the forensics doctor, asking him to call him.

'I am writing up my report, which you'll have tomorrow morning,' said the handsomely bearded doctor, who would have another post mortem to perform that evening. 'I wanted to bring a couple of things to your attention, as they may be important for your investigation. First, everything suggests the girl isn't twenty-four, as it says on her card. Medically speaking she is barely twenty.'

'Are you sure?'

'It's a near certainty. What's more, she has had a child. That's all I know. As for the murder, it was carried out by somebody very strong.'

'Could a woman have done it?'

'I don't think so, unless she was physically as powerful as a man.'

'Has anyone told you about the second crime yet? You're most probably going to be called out to Rue Victor-Massé.'

Doctor Paul muttered something about a dinner in town, and the two men hung up.

The evening papers had published Arlette's photograph and, as per normal, they had already received several telephone calls. Two or three people were in the waiting room. An inspector was dealing with it all, and Maigret went to have dinner at home, where his wife, who had read the newspaper, wasn't expecting to see him. It was still raining. His clothes were damp, and he changed.

'Are you going out?'

'I'll probably be gone for the better part of the night.'

'Has the countess been found?'

The newspapers hadn't mentioned the dead woman in Rue Victor-Massé yet.

'Yes. Strangled.'

'Don't catch cold. The radio's saying there's going to be a frost and that it'll probably be icy tomorrow morning.'

He drank a little brandy and walked to Place de la République to get some fresh air.

His initial plan had been to let young Lapointe deal with Arlette, but, on reflection, entrusting him with this job seemed cruel, and he'd ended up giving it to Janvier.

The latter should be at work now. Equipped with a photograph of the dancer, he would be going around Montmartre's boarding houses, concentrating in particular on those little hotels that specialize in letting out rooms by the hour.

Fred from Picratt's had implied that, like the other dancers, Arlette would sometimes go off with a customer after the club closed. She didn't take them home, according to the concierge of Rue Notre-Dame-de-Lorette. She wouldn't have gone very far. Maybe, if she had a regular lover, she would have met up with him in one of these hotels too.

While he was at it, Janvier was primed to ask everyone about an Oscar, who they knew nothing about and whose name had only been uttered once by the young woman.

Why had she seemed to regret it instantly and become much vaguer?

Short on manpower, Maigret had left Inspector Lognon at Rue Victor-Massé, where Criminal Records should have finished its work by now and where the public prosecutor would probably have put in an appearance while he was having dinner.

When he got to Quai des Orfèvres, most of the offices were dark and he found Lapointe in the big inspectors' room, bent over the papers from the countess's drawer. He had been given the job of sorting through them.

'Have you found anything, son?'

'I'm not finished. All of this is a mess, and it's not easy getting your bearings. Plus I'm checking things as I go along. I've already made some calls. I'm waiting to hear from the Flying Squad in Nice, apart from anything else.'

He produced a postcard of a sprawling, luxurious estate overlooking the Baie des Anges. The house, a bad Orientalist pastiche complete with minaret, was surrounded by palm trees and its name was printed in the corner: The Oasis.

'According to the papers,' he explained, 'this is where she lived with her husband fifteen years ago.'

'So she was under thirty-five then.'

'Here's a photograph of her and the count at the time.'

It was a snapshot. They were both standing in front of the door of the villa, and the woman was holding two huge borzois on leads.

Count von Farnheim was a trim little man with a white goatee, dressed with studied elegance and sporting a monocle. His wife was a beautiful, voluptuous creature who must have turned heads in the street.

'Do you know where they got married?'

'In Capri, three years before that photograph was taken.'

'How old was the count?'

'Sixty-five when they got married. The marriage only lasted three years. He bought The Oasis as soon as they got back from Italy.'

The papers contained a bit of everything: yellowing bills, passports with multiple visas, cards from Nice's and Cannes' casinos, even a bundle of letters which Lapointe hadn't yet had time to decipher. They were in an angular hand, with some letters in Gothic script, and signed Hans.

'Do you know her maiden name?'

'Madeleine Lalande. She was born in La Roche-sur-Yon, in the Vendée, and for a while was one of the extras at the Casino de Paris.'

Lapointe regarded his job more or less as a form of punishment.

'Haven't we found anything?' he asked after a silence.

He was obviously thinking about Arlette.

'Janvier's taking care of it. I will as well.'

'Are you going to Picratt's?'

Maigret nodded. In his office next door, he found the inspector who was dealing with the telephone calls and visits concerning the dancer's identity.

'Nothing serious yet. I took an old woman, who seemed very self-assured, to the Forensic Institute. Even when she was standing in front of the body, she swore it was her daughter, but the clerk there identified her. She's mad.

She's been recognizing every woman's body that's turned up for the last ten years.'

The meteorological office must have got it right for once, because when Maigret was back outside, it was colder, a wintry cold, and he turned up the collar of his overcoat. He got to Montmartre too early. It was just after eleven, and the nightlife hadn't started. People were still crammed shoulder to shoulder in the theatres and cinemas; the cabarets were only just switching on their neon signs, and the liveried doormen weren't at their stations yet.

First he went into the café-tabac on the corner of Rue de Douai. He had been there countless times, and they knew him. The owner had only just started work because he was another nighthawk . His wife ran the bar in the day with a team of waiters until he relieved her in the evening, so they only saw each other in passing.

'What can I get you, inspector?'

Maigret immediately noticed a character whom the owner seemed to be indicating out of the corner of his eye. It was obviously the Grasshopper. He was standing at the bar, his head barely reaching over the counter, drinking a peppermint cordial. He had recognized Maigret too but was pretending to be immersed in a racing paper, which he was marking up in pencil.

He could have been taken for a jockey because he must have been the weight for it. When you looked at him closely, it was disorientating to discover on that childlike body a grey, wrinkled face with intensely animated, darting eyes that seemed to register everything, like an animal always on the alert.

He was wearing a suit rather than a uniform, which on him looked like something a teenager would wear to his first communion.

'Were you working about four this morning?' Maigret asked the owner after ordering a calvados.

'Same as every night. I know what you're driving at. I've read the paper.'

People like him made Maigret's job easy. A few musicians were drinking a café-crème before going to work. There were also a couple of young thugs whom he knew, who were trying to look innocent.

'What sort of state was she in?'

'Same as she always was at that time of the morning.'

'Did she come every night?'

'No. Every now and then. When she thought she hadn't had her fill. She'd have one or two drinks, stiff ones, then head home. She wouldn't hang around.'

'Last night was the same?'

'She seemed pretty worked up, but she didn't say anything to me. I don't think she talked to anyone apart from to order her drink.'

'Was there a middle-aged man, short and burly, with grey hair, in the bar?'

Maigret had avoided talking about Oscar to the reporters, so there hadn't been any mention of him in the newspapers. But he had asked Fred about him; Fred might have repeated his questions to the Grasshopper, and he . . .

'No, no sign of anyone like that,' replied the bar owner, perhaps a shade too emphatically.

'You don't know anyone called Oscar?'

'There are loads of Oscars around here, but I can't think of one that fits that description.'

Maigret was at the Grasshopper's side in a couple of steps.

'Nothing to tell me?'

'Nothing special, inspector.'

'You spent all last night on the door at Picratt's?'

'Pretty much. I just went a little way up Rue Pigalle once or twice, handing out cards. I came in here too, to get some cigarettes for an American.'

'Do you know Oscar?'

'Never heard of him.'

He wasn't the sort of guy to be intimidated by the police, or anyone, for that matter. His broad working-class accent and street-kid mannerisms were clearly intentional, part of a whole act that went down well with the customers.

'You didn't know Arlette's boyfriend either?'

'She had a boyfriend? First I've heard of it.'

'You never saw anyone waiting for her afterwards?'

'Sometimes. Customers.'

'Would she go off with them?'

'Not always. Occasionally she had a hard time getting rid of them and had to come in here to shake them off.'

The owner, who was shamelessly listening in, nodded in agreement.

'You never ran into her in the day?'

'Mornings I'm asleep and afternoons I'm at the track.'

'She didn't have any girlfriends?'

'She got on with Betty and Tania. Not all that well. I think Tania and her weren't too fond of each other.'

'She never asked you to get her drugs?'

'Why?'

'For her.'

'Not a chance. She liked having a drink, or even a couple, but I don't think she ever took drugs.'

'In a word, you don't know anything.'

'Except that she was the most beautiful girl I've ever seen.'

Maigret hesitated, involuntarily looking the runt up and down from head to toe.

'Did you go to bed with her?'

'Why not? I've had my way with others, and not just kids either. High-class customers too.'

'It's perfectly true,' put in the proprietor. 'I don't know what's the matter with them, but they're all crazy about him. I've seen some women – not old or ugly by any stretch of the imagination – come in here at the end of the night and wait for him for at least an hour.'

The gnome's big, rubbery mouth stretched into a sardonic, delighted smile.

'Maybe there's a good reason for it,' he said, making an obscene gesture.

'You slept with Arlette?'

'I already said I did.'

'Often?'

'Once, at least.'

'Was it her idea?'

'She knew I wanted it.'

'Where did it happen?'

'Not at Picratt's, obviously. Do you know the Moderne on Rue Blanche?'

It was a hotel used by prostitutes that the police knew well.

'Well, it was there.'

'Was she passionate?'

'She knew all the tricks.'

'Did she like it?'

The Grasshopper shrugged.

'Even when women don't like it, they pretend to, and the less pleasure they get, the more of a show they think they have to put on.'

'Was she drunk that night?'

'Same as always.'

'Was she like that with the owner too?'

'With Fred? He's talked to you about it?'

He thought for a minute, then gravely drained his drink.

'That's none of my business.'

'Do you think the boss fell for her?'

'Everyone fell for her.'

'You too?'

'I've said what I had to say. Now, I can always do you a drawing, if you'd like,' he joked. 'Are you going to Picratt's?'

Maigret headed off there without waiting for the Grasshopper, who wasted no time taking up his post. The red sign was on. The photographs of Arlette hadn't been removed from the display yet. A curtain was drawn across the window and the glass panes of the door. There was no music to be heard.

He went in and the first thing he saw was Fred in a dinner-jacket, shelving some bottles behind the bar.

'I thought you'd show up,' he said. 'Is it true that a countess has been found strangled?'

It wasn't surprising he knew. It had happened in the neighbourhood, after all. It might have been on the radio as well.

Two musicians, one very young with slicked-back hair, another in his forties with a sad, sickly air, were sitting on stage, tuning up. A waiter was finishing the tables. There was no sign of Rose, who must have been in the kitchen or had not come down yet.

The walls were painted red, the lighting was deep pink, and the combination made everything – objects as well as people – seem a little less real. You felt – or at least Maigret felt – as if you were in a photographer's dark room. He needed a moment to adjust. People's eyes appeared darker, more sparkling, while the outline of their lips disappeared, swallowed up by the light.

'If you're staying, give your coat and hat to my wife. You'll find her at the back.'

He called:

'Rose!'

She came out of the kitchen, wearing a black satin dress and, on top of it, a little embroidered apron. She took his overcoat and hat.

'I suppose you don't want to sit down straight away?'

'Have the women got here?'

'They'll be down. They're changing. We don't have artists' dressing rooms here, so they use our bedroom and bathroom. I've been having a good think about the questions you asked me this morning, you know. We talked it over, Rose and me. We're both sure that Arlette can't have found out from overhearing customers. Come here, Désiré.'

The latter was bald, apart from a ring of hair around his head, and looked like the waiter in a poster for a big drinks company. He must have known it and cultivated the resemblance; he had even let his sideburns grow.

'You can speak openly to the inspector. Did you serve any customers on four last night?'

'No, monsieur.'

'Did you see two men together – they would have been here a while – one of them a short, middle-aged guy?'

After a glance at Maigret, Fred added, 'Who looked a bit like me?'

'No, monsieur.'

'Who did Arlette talk to?'

'She was with her young man for quite a long time. Then she took a few glasses to the Americans' table. That's it. At the end she was sitting with Betty, and they ordered brandy from me. It went on her tab. You can check. She drank a couple of glasses.'

A dark-haired woman came out of the kitchen and after a professional scan of the room, in which the only strange face was Maigret's, headed towards the stage, sat down at the piano and spoke quietly to the musicians. All three looked in Maigret's direction. Then she gave her companions a chord. The younger man produced a few notes from his saxophone, the other sat down at the drums, and, moments later, a jazz tune struck up.

'People passing by have got to hear music,' Fred explained. 'There probably won't be anyone for a good half-hour but a customer mustn't find the club silent or us frozen like waxworks. What can I give you? If you're sitting down, I'd rather it was a bottle of champagne.'

'I'd prefer a brandy.'

'I'll give you a glass of brandy and put the bottle of champagne next to it. As a rule, especially at the start of the night, we only serve champagne, you understand?'

He did his job with palpable satisfaction, as if he was fulfilling his life's dream. He kept an eye on everything. His wife had already taken up position on a chair at the back of the room, behind the musicians, and that seemed to please both of them. They had probably dreamed of starting their own business for a long time, and it still felt like a sort of game to them.

'Right, I'll put you at table six, where Arlette and her lover were sitting. If you want to talk to Tania, wait until they play a java. Jean-Jean gets on the accordion for those, and she can have a break from the piano. We used to have a pianist before. Then, when we'd taken her on and I knew she played, I thought it would save us money using her in the band. Here's Betty coming down. Shall I introduce her to you?'

Maigret had sat down in the booth like a customer, and Fred brought over a young girl with reddish hair who was wearing a sequined dress that glinted blue in the light.

'Detective Chief Inspector Maigret, who's looking into Arlette's death. You needn't be afraid. He's above board.'

He might have found her pretty if he hadn't sensed her body was hard and muscled like a man's. It was disconcerting: she might almost have been mistaken for a teenager in drag. Even her voice was deep, slightly hoarse.

'Do you want me to sit down at your table?'

'Please. Will you have something?'

'I'd rather not for now. Désiré will put a glass in front of me. That'll do.'

She seemed weary, anxious. It was hard to think she was there to excite men, and she can't have been too optimistic herself.

'Are you Belgian?' he asked because of her accent.

'I'm from Anderlecht, near Brussels. Before coming here, I was in an acrobatic troupe. I started very young; my father was in a circus.'

'How old are you?'

'Twenty-eight. I got too rusty for that line of work, so I started dancing.'

'Married?'

'I was, to a juggler who ditched me.'

'Did Arlette leave with you last night?'

'Same as every night. Tania lives over by Gare Saint-Lazare and takes Rue Pigalle. She's always ready before us. I live just round the corner, and Arlette and me always used to say goodnight on the corner of Rue Notre-Dame-de-Lorette.'

'Did she go straight to her place?'

'No. She did that sometimes. She'd pretend to turn right, then, as soon as I was out of sight, I'd hear her going back up the street to have a drink at the tabac on Rue de Douai.'

'Why did she keep it secret?'

'People who drink generally don't like you seeing them chasing off after a last drink.'

'Had she drunk a lot?'

'She drank two brandies before leaving, with me, and she'd already had loads of champagne. I'm sure she'd started before she even came to work as well.'

'Was she sad about anything?'

'If she was, she didn't tell me. I think she was just sick and tired.'

Betty might have been a bit sick and tired herself because she said this gloomily, her voice an indifferent monotone.

'What do you know about her?'

Two customers had just come in, a man and a woman, whom Désiré was trying to manoeuvre to a table. Seeing the empty room, they hesitated, looked questioningly at each other. Then the man said, embarrassed:

'We'll come back.'

'Some people who got the wrong floor,' Betty remarked calmly. 'Not for us.'

She made an attempt at a smile.

'It'll be a good hour before it gets going. Sometimes we start our acts with only three customers watching.'

'Why had Arlette chosen this line of work?'

She looked at him for a long time, then muttered:

'I often asked her that. I've no idea. Maybe because she liked it?'

She glanced at the photographs on the walls.

'You know what it was like, her act? I doubt they'll ever find anybody who can bring it off the way she did. It looks easy. We've all tried it. But I can tell you it's unbelievably hard. Because if it's just done any old how, it looks sleazy straight away. You've really got to look as if you're doing it because you get a kick out of it.'

'Did Arlette give that impression?'

'I sometimes wondered if that wasn't why she did it in the first place! I'm not saying because she desired men. She may easily not have. But she needed to turn them on, keep them in suspense. When she finished and came back into the kitchen – that's our wings, because we go through there to go upstairs and change – when she'd finish, as I was saying, she'd open the door and peek through to see how she'd gone down, like an actor who looks through a peephole in the curtain.'

'Was she in love with anyone?'

She was silent for a while.

'Maybe,' she said finally. 'Yesterday morning I would have said she wasn't. But last night, when her young man left, she seemed on edge. She said that she was an idiot, really. I asked her why. She said it was completely up to her whether things changed or not. "What?" I asked.

'"Everything! I'm sick of it."

'"Do you want to leave the club?"

'We were whispering in case Fred heard. She answered:

'"The club's not the only thing in the world!"

'She'd been drinking, I know, but I'm sure there was something to what she was saying.

'"Has he said he wants to support you?"

'She shrugged her shoulders and changed the subject.

'"You wouldn't even understand."

'We almost had an argument, and I told her to her face that I wasn't as stupid as she thought, that I'd gone through the same thing myself.'

This time the Grasshopper was triumphantly showing in some genuine customers. It was three men and a woman. The men were obviously foreigners, who, judging by their self-important air, were probably in Paris on business or for a conference. As for the woman, heaven knows where they had picked her up, sitting outside a café probably. She looked a little embarrassed.

With a wink at Maigret, Fred sat them at number four and gave them an enormous menu on which was listed every conceivable type of champagne. The cellar can't have contained a quarter of them, and Fred recommended a completely unknown brand which he must have marked up 300 per cent.

'I'm going to have to get ready for my act,' sighed Betty. 'Don't expect anything out of this world, but it's still good enough for them. All they ask for is a little bit of thigh!'

The band played a java, and Maigret signalled to Tania, who had stepped off the stage, to come and join him. Fred gave her a look indicating that she should go.

'Do you want to talk to me?'

She didn't have a Russian accent, despite her name, and Maigret learned that she had been born in Rue Mouffetard.

'Sit down and tell me what you know about Arlette.'

'We weren't friends.'

'Why?'

'I didn't like her attitude.'

The statement rang out like a slap. She clearly thought she was somebody, and Maigret didn't remotely impress her.

'Did you argue?'

'It didn't go that far.'

'Did you talk sometimes?'

'As little as possible. She was jealous.'

'Of what?'

'Of me. She couldn't get it into her head that another woman could be attractive. No one else existed except her. I don't like that. She couldn't even dance, had never had lessons. All she could do was take her clothes off, and if she hadn't shown them everything, she wouldn't have had an act.'

'Are you a dancer?'

'I was studying classical ballet by the time I was twelve.'

'Is that what you dance here?'

'No. Here I do Russian dances.'

'Did Arlette have a lover?'

'Yes, probably, but she must have had good reason not to be proud of the fact. That's why she never talked about him. All I can tell you is that it was an old man.'

'How do you know that?'

'We all get changed together up there. I saw bruises on her body a few times. She tried to hide them under a layer of cold cream, but I've got good eyes.'

'Did you talk to her about it?'

'Once. She told me she had fallen down the stairs. But she can't have fallen down the stairs every week. I figured it out from where the bruises were. Only old men have those vices.'

'When did you first notice it?'

'Six months ago, at least, almost straight after I started.'

'And it carried on?'

'I didn't look at her every evening but I often saw bruises. Is there anything else you want to say to me? I've got to get back to the piano.'

She had barely sat down before the lights went out and a spotlight lit up the dance-floor as Betty Bruce came bounding out. Maigret heard voices behind him: men's voices trying to express themselves in French and a woman's voice who was teaching them how to pronounce *'Voulez-vous coucher avec moi?'*

They were laughing, practising in turn:

'Vo-lez vo . . .'

Without saying a word, Fred, whose shirtfront stood out in the dark, came and sat down facing Maigret. More or less in time with the music, Betty Bruce lifted one leg at a perfect right angle while jiggling around on the other, her stockings stretched tight, her mouth frozen in a smile, then sank to the ground in the splits.

5.

When his wife woke him with his cup of coffee, Maigret immediately knew that he hadn't slept enough and that he had a headache, then he opened his eyes and wondered why Madame Maigret was so cheery, like someone with a wonderful surprise up her sleeve.

'Look!' she said, when he had grasped the cup in a not yet very steady hand.

She pulled the curtain cord, and he saw that it was snowing.

'Aren't you pleased?'

Naturally he was pleased, but his furred tongue suggested he had drunk more than he had realized. This was probably because Désiré, the waiter, had opened the bottle of champagne, which was theoretically only there for show, and he had unthinkingly helped himself to it between brandies.

'I don't know if it will settle, but it's still more cheerful than rain!'

Actually, it didn't really matter to Maigret whether it was cheerful or not. He liked all kinds of weather. He liked extreme weather the most, the sort that would earn a mention in the paper the following day, torrential rain, tornadoes, bitter cold or torrid heat. He enjoyed the snow too because it reminded him of his childhood, but he wondered how his wife could find it cheerful in Paris, especially on a morning like this. The sky was even more leaden than the day before, and the white snowflakes made the glistening black roofs even blacker, bringing out the sad, dirty colour of the houses, the questionable cleanliness of the curtains in the windows.

It took him a while, as he had his breakfast and got dressed, to get his memories of the previous night in some sort of order. He had only had a few hours' sleep. When he had left Picratt's at closing time, it was at least half past four in the morning, and he had thought it necessary to imitate Arlette and go and have one last drink at the tabac on Rue de Douai.

He would have found it hard to sum up what he'd learned in a few words. A lot of the time he had been alone in his booth, taking small puffs on his pipe, watching the dance-floor or the clientele, all bathed in that strange light that took you away from real life.

All in all, he could have left earlier. He stayed on out of laziness, and also because there was something about the atmosphere that kept him there, because he enjoyed studying the people, the little tricks of the owner, Rose and the girls.

It was a little universe living, as it were, in complete ignorance of the wider world. Everyone – Désiré, the two musicians, all the others – went to bed when alarm clocks were going off in regular homes and spent most of their days asleep. And that's how Arlette had lived, only really starting to wake up under the reddish glow of Picratt's lights and coming into contact with virtually no one other than drunk men who had been picked up by the Grasshopper as they were leaving other clubs.

Maigret watched Betty's performance. Aware of his attention, she seemed to make a point of pulling out all the stops for him, and occasionally tipped him a complicit wink.

Two customers had arrived at about three o'clock after she had finished and gone upstairs to get dressed. They were roaring drunk and, as the club was a bit dead just then, Fred headed for the kitchen. Presumably he went up to tell Betty to come back down quick smart.

She had started her act again, but this time she performed it just for the two men, lifting her leg right in front of their noses and rounding it off with a kiss on the bald patch of one of them. Before she went and changed, she sat on the other's lap and drank a mouthful of champagne from his glass.

Was that Arlette's approach too? A subtler version, probably?

The men spoke a little French, very little. She repeated, 'Cinq minutes . . . Cinq minutes . . . Moi revenir . . .'

She held up five fingers and did in fact then come back a few minutes later, in her sequined dress, and peremptorily called to Désiré to bring another bottle.

Meanwhile Tania was busy with a solitary customer who had turned maudlin after a few drinks and, with a hand on her bare knee, was no doubt pouring out confidences about his marriage.

The two Dutchmen's hands were never still, always somewhere else on Betty's body. They laughed loudly, becoming ever redder in the face, as bottle after bottle appeared on their table, was drunk and then stashed underneath it. Eventually Maigret realized that some of these empty bottles had never been full in the first place. That was the scam, as Fred admitted with a look.

At one point, Maigret went to the toilet. There was an outer room with combs, brushes, face-powder and make-up in a row on a shelf. Rose followed him in there.

'I've thought of something that might be of use to you,' she said. 'Just now when I saw you come in here, in fact. This is generally where the girls confide in me, while they're smartening themselves up. Arlette wasn't a talker, but she still told me some things, and I guessed others.'

She handed him the soap and a clean towel.

'She couldn't have been from the same background as the rest of us. She didn't talk to me about her family, I don't think she did to anyone, but she mentioned the convent where she was educated several times.'

'Do you remember what she said?'

'If ever a hard, mean woman came up in conversation, especially one of those ones who seem kind and then stick the knife in on the sly, she'd mutter – and you could tell she was really upset – "She sounds like Mother Eudice." I asked her who that was, and she said she was the person she hated most in the whole world, the one who had hurt her more than anyone else. She was the Mother Superior of the convent, and she'd suddenly taken against Arlette. I remember her also saying: "I would have gone bad just to annoy her."'

'She didn't say which convent it was?'

'No, but it can't have been far from the sea, because she talked about the sea a few times like someone who had grown up by it.'

It was funny. As she was talking, Rose treated Maigret as a customer, automatically brushing his back and shoulders.

'I think she loathed her mother too. That's vaguer. It's one of those things a woman senses. One evening, we had some very well-to-do people in who were painting the town red, especially a minister's wife who really looked like a very grand lady. She seemed sad, preoccupied, took no interest in the show, sipped at her drink and barely listened to what her friends were saying. I knew her story, so I said to Arlette, again in here, while she was fixing her make-up, "You've got to give her her due, because she's had one terrible thing happen to her after another."

'Then she replied spitefully, "I don't trust people who've had troubles, especially women. They use it as an excuse to trample all over everyone else."

'It's only a hunch, but I'd swear she meant her mother. She never talked about her father. When you said that word, she'd look the other way.

'That's all I know. I always thought she was a girl from a good family who had rebelled. They're the worst, when they get the bit between their teeth, and it explains a lot of things.'

'You mean her urge to arouse men?'

'Yes. And the way she went about it. I wasn't born yesterday. I was in this game in the past, and worse, as you probably know. But not like her. That's exactly why she's irreplaceable. The real ones, the professionals, never put as much passion into it. Have a look at the other girls. Even when they let rip, you can feel their heart isn't really in it . . .'

Now and then Fred would come and sit down at Maigret's table for a moment and exchange a few words with him. Each time, Désiré would bring two brandies and water, but Maigret noticed that the owner's was always a lighter colour. He drank and thought about Arlette, and Lapointe, who had been sitting in that booth with her the night before.

Inspector Lognon was dealing with the countess, who didn't interest Maigret much at all. He had known too many of her kind, women past their prime, almost always single, almost always trailing a glittering past, who were mixed up with drugs and sinking into abject ruin. There were maybe 200 like her in Montmartre, and on the next rung up, a few dozen in the swish apartments of Passy and Auteuil.

Arlette was the one who interested him, because he still hadn't managed to place her or really understand her.

'Was she passionate?' he asked Fred once.

The latter shrugged.

'You know, I don't bother my head too much about them. My wife told you that yesterday, and it's true. I meet up with them in the kitchen, or I go upstairs when they're changing. I don't ask them what they think about it, and it never means anything.'

'Did you ever see her outside the club?'

'In the street?'

'No, I'm asking you if you ever met up with her.'

Maigret had a feeling he hesitated, glancing towards the back of the room, where his wife was sitting.

'No,' he said finally.

He was lying. That was the first thing Maigret discovered when he got to Quai des Orfèvres, where he was late and had missed the briefing. The inspectors' office was bustling. He telephoned the chief first to apologize and tell him he would see him as soon as he had questioned his men.

When he rang the bell, Janvier and Lapointe both appeared at his door.

'Janvier first,' he said. 'I'll call you in a minute, Lapointe.'

Janvier looked as dazed as he did and had clearly been trailing around the streets for most of the night.

'I thought you might come and see me at Picratt's.'

'I meant to. But the further I went, the more work I had. In the end I never got to bed.'

'Found Oscar?'

Janvier took a piece of paper covered with notes out of his pocket.

'I don't know. I don't think so. I covered pretty much all the rooms to rent between Rue Châteaudun and the Montmartre boulevards. I showed the photo of the girl in every hotel. Some of the managers pretended not to recognize her or gave evasive answers.'

'And?'

'In ten of those hotels, at least, they knew her.'

'Did you try to find out if she was ever with the same man?'

'I made a point of asking that. Apparently she wasn't. Most of the time, she went around four or five in the morning, with people pretty far gone on drink, probably customers from Picratt's.'

'Did she stay long?'

'Never more than an hour or two.'

'Did you find out if she got paid?'

'When I asked, the hoteliers looked at me as if I was from another planet. Twice, at the Moderne, she went up with a young man with slicked-back hair carrying a saxophone case under his arm.'

'Jean-Jean, the musician from the club.'

'Possibly. The last time was about a fortnight ago. You know the Hôtel du Berry on Rue Blanche? It's not far from Picratt's and Rue Notre-Dame-de-Lorette. She often went there. The owner is very forthcoming, because she's already been in trouble with us over underage girls and wants to get in our good books. Arlette went in one afternoon, a few weeks ago, with a short, square-shouldered man who was greying at the temples.'

'The woman doesn't know him?'

'She thinks she knows him by sight, but not who he is. She claims he's almost definitely from the neighbourhood. They stayed in the room until nine in the evening. She was struck by that because Arlette almost never came in the day or evening but, most of all, because she usually left almost immediately.'

'Get a photograph of Fred Alfonsi and show it to her.'

Janvier, who didn't know Picratt's owner, frowned.

'If it's him, Arlette met up with him somewhere else as well. Hang on, I'll check the list . . . At the Hôtel Lepic, Rue Lepic. A man was on reception there, a guy with one leg who spends his nights reading novels and says he can't sleep because his leg hurts. He recognized her. She went there several times, in particular, he said, with someone who he's often seen at the market on Rue Lepic, but whose name he doesn't know. A short, burly man who would usually do his shopping in the late morning without bothering to put on a shirt collar, as if he was just going round the corner. That sounds right, doesn't it?'

'It's possible. You're going to have to go round again with a photograph of Alfonsi. There's one in the file but it's too old.'

'Can I ask him for one?'

'Just ask him for his identity card as if you're going to check it and get the photo copied upstairs.'

The office boy came in and announced that a lady wanted to speak to Maigret.

'Ask her to wait. I'll be there in a minute.'

Janvier added:

'Marcoussis is going through the post. Apparently there's loads of letters about Arlette's identity. This morning he got twenty or so telephone calls. We're checking, but I don't think there's anything serious yet.'

'Did you talk to everybody about Oscar?'

'Yes. No one turns a hair. Or they run through the Oscars in the neighbourhood, none of whom fits the description.'

'Send Lapointe in.'

The latter looked anxious. He knew that the two men had just been talking about Arlette and wondered why, for the first time ever, he hadn't been allowed to listen in on their conversation.

The inquiring look he gave Maigret was almost beseeching.

'Sit down, son. If there were any news, I would tell you. We've barely made any progress since yesterday.'

'Did you spend the night there?'

'In the same seat you were in the night before, yes. Incidentally, did she ever talk to you about her family?'

'All I know is that she ran away from home.'

'She didn't tell you why?'

'She told me that she loathed hypocrisy, that she'd felt she was suffocating all her childhood.'

'Be straight with me: was she kind to you?'

'What do you mean exactly?'

'Did she treat you as a friend? Was she honest with you?'

'At times, yes, I think so. It's hard to explain.'

'Did you flirt with her immediately?'

'I told her I loved her.'

'The first evening?'

'No. The first evening, I was with my friend and practically didn't open my mouth. It was when I went back on my own.'

'What did she say?'

'She tried to treat me as a kid and I said that I was twenty-four and that I was older than her.

'"It's not the years that count, sweetheart," she snapped. "I am so much older than you!"

'You see, she was very sad: desperate even, I'd say. I think that's why I loved her. She laughed and joked, but it was all so bitter. There were times . . .'

'Go on.'

'I know you think I'm naive, like everybody else. She tried to push me away, made a point of being vulgar, using crude language.

'"Why don't you just sleep with me like the rest? Don't I turn you on? I could teach you more than any ordinary woman. I bet you won't find anyone as experienced as me, who can do it the way I can . . ."'

'Wait! It suddenly occurs to me what she said next:

'"I was well schooled."'

'You never wanted to give it a try?'

'I wanted her. At times I could have shouted it out. But I didn't want her like that. It would have ruined everything, do you see?'

'I do. And what did she say when you talked about her starting a new life?'

'She laughed, calling me her little virgin, and began drinking even harder. I am sure it was out of despair. You haven't found the man?'

'Which man?'

'The one she called Oscar.'

'We haven't got anywhere yet. Now, tell me about what you did last night.'

Lapointe had brought a bulging folder containing the papers they had found at the countess's. He had carefully sorted them and covered several pages with notes.

'I've been able to piece together almost all the countess's life,' he said. 'The Nice police reported to me by telephone this morning.'

'Let's hear it.'

'First I know her real name: Madeleine Lalande.'

'I saw that on the family register yesterday.'

'That's true. Sorry. She was born at La Roche-sur-Yon, where her mother was a domestic. She didn't know her father. She came to Paris as a chambermaid, but somebody was already keeping her after a few months. She changed lover several times, climbing the ladder a little with each one, and fifteen years ago she was considered one of the most beautiful women on the Côte d'Azur.'

'Was she already on drugs?'

'I've no idea but I haven't found anything that would suggest it. She gambled, hung around the casinos. She met Count von Farnheim, from an old Austrian family, who was then sixty-five. The count's letters are here, arranged by date.'

'Have you read them all?'

'Yes. He was passionately in love with her.'

Lapointe blushed, as if he could have written the letters himself.

'They are very moving. He realized that he was just an old, all but impotent man. The first letters are respectful. He calls her "madame", then "my dear friend", then finally "my darling little girl", begs her not to abandon him, never to leave him on his own. He keeps telling her that she's all

97

he's got in the world and that he can't conceive of spending his last years without her.'

'Did they sleep together immediately?'

'No. It took months. He fell sick, in a furnished villa he lived in before buying The Oasis, and he got her to come and live there as a guest and grace him with a few hours of her presence. You feel that he is sincere in every line, that he is desperately clinging on to her, that he'll do anything not to lose her. He talks bitterly about the age difference, tells her that he knows he's not offering her an agreeable life. "It won't be for long," he writes at one point. 'I am old, my health is bad. In a few years, you will be free, my little girl, still beautiful, and if you permit it, you will be rich . . ." He writes to her every day, sometimes schoolboyish little notes: "I love you! I love you! I love you!" Then suddenly it's pure rapture, a sort of Song of Songs. The tone has changed, and he talks about her body with a mixture of passion and something like reverence. "I cannot believe that that body has been mine, that those breasts, those hips, that belly . . ."'

Maigret looked thoughtfully at Lapointe and did not smile.

'From then on he is haunted by the thought that he might lose her. At the same time, he is tortured by jealousy. He begs her to tell him everything, even if the truth is bound to hurt him. He asks what she did the night before, which men she talked to. There are references to a musician at the casino who he thinks is too good-looking and is terribly afraid of. He also wants to know about her past. "It's 'the whole you' I need . . ." Finally he begs her to marry him. I haven't got any of her letters. She seems not to have written back but either to have answered him in person or telephoned. In one of the last notes, where his age comes up again, the count bursts out: "I should have realized that your beautiful body has needs I cannot satisfy. It's torture. Each time I think about it, it hurts me so much I think I am dying. But I'd rather share you than not have you at all. I swear I will never make a scene or reproach you. You will be as free as you are today and I, in my corner, I'll be waiting for you to bring a little joy to your old husband . . ."'

Lapointe blew his nose.

'They went to Capri to get married, I don't know why. There wasn't a marriage contract, so they observed the laws of common property. They travelled for several months, went to Constantinople and Cairo, then set themselves up for several weeks in a luxury hotel on the Champs-Élysées. I know because I found some hotel bills.'

'When did he die?'

'The Nice police were able to fill me in. Barely three years after he got married. They had moved into The Oasis. For months on end people saw them in a chauffeur-driven limousine, shuttling between the casinos of Monte-Carlo, Cannes and Juan-les-Pins. She was sumptuously dressed, dripping in jewels. Their arrival would cause a sensation, because she was hard to miss, and her husband was always in her wake, small and sickly, with a black goatee and pince-nez. He was known as the rat. She gambled for high stakes, had no qualms about flirting, and people say that she had a certain number of affairs.

Meanwhile he would wait, like her shadow, until the early hours of the morning with a resigned smile.'

'How did he die?'

'Nice is going to send you the report by post, because there was an inquiry. The Oasis is on the Corniche, and the terrace, which is lined with palm trees, overlooks a sheer drop of hundreds of metres, like most of the properties around there. The count's body was found one morning at the foot of the cliff.'

'Did he drink?'

'He was on the wagon. His doctor stated that because of certain medicines he had to take he suffered from dizzy spells.'

'Did the count and countess share a bedroom?'

'Each of them had their own apartments. The previous evening they had gone to the casino as usual and come back around three in the morning, which, for them, was exceptionally early. The countess was tired. She gave a candid explanation of why to the police: it was her time of the month and she was in a lot of pain. She went straight to bed. Her husband, meanwhile, according to the chauffeur, first went down to the library, which has French windows giving on to the terrace. He sometimes did that when he had insomnia. He didn't sleep much. The assumption is that he wanted to get some air and sat down on the stone parapet. It was his favourite spot because, from there, you could see the Baie des Anges, the lights of Nice and much of the coast. When he was found, the body bore no marks of violence and the subsequent post-mortem was inconclusive.'

'What did she do after that?'

'She had a big fight with a great nephew, who turned up from Austria and sued her, and it took her almost two years to win the day. She carried on living in Nice, in The Oasis. She entertained a lot. Her house was very wild, and the drinking used to go on all night. Often the guests would sleep there, and the party would start up again when they woke up. According to the police there was a succession of gigolos, and they relieved her of a good chunk of her money. I wondered if that was when she starting taking drugs heavily, but they couldn't tell me anything specific. They're going to try to find out, but all this is already pretty old news. The only report they've found so far leaves lots of gaps, and they're not sure they'll be able to track down the file. What we know is that she drank and gambled. When she was drunk she'd take everyone back to her house. You get the picture? Apparently there's a fair few oddballs like her down there. She must have lost a lot of money at roulette, where she'd sometimes bet the same number for hours at a time. Four years after her husband died, she sold The Oasis and, as it was in the middle of the crash, she didn't get a good price for it. I think that it's a sanatorium or a rest home these days. At any rate it's not a private house any more. That's all Nice knows. Once the estate was sold, the countess dropped out of sight and she was never seen on the Côte d'Azur again.'

'You should stop by the Gambling Squad,' Maigret advised. 'Drugs may have something to tell you too.'

'Aren't I on Arlette's case?'

'Not for now. I'd like you to call Nice again as well. They may be able to give you a list of everyone who was living at The Oasis when the count died. Don't forget the staff. Even though it was fifteen years ago, we might still be able to track some of them down.'

It was still snowing fairly thickly, but the flakes were so light and wispy that they melted the moment they touched a wall or the ground.

'Anything else, chief?'

'Not at the moment. Leave me the file.'

'You don't want me to write up my report?'

'Not until it's over. Off you go!'

Maigret stood up, drowsy from the heat of the office, still with a bad taste in his mouth and a dull pain at the base of his skull. He remembered that a woman was waiting for him in the anteroom, and to stretch his legs decided to fetch her himself. If he'd had time, he would have nipped down to the Brasserie Dauphine for a glass of beer, which would have perked him up.

Several people were sitting in the glassed-in waiting room, where the green of the chairs looked more garish than usual and an umbrella was standing in a puddle of water in the corner. He looked to see who was waiting for him and spotted a middle-aged woman in black, sitting very upright on a chair, who stood up when he came in. No doubt she had seen his picture in the papers.

Lognon, meanwhile, who was there too, didn't get up, didn't move, but just looked at Maigret with a sigh. Typical. He needed to feel intensely unfortunate, intensely hard-done-by, to see himself as a victim of cruel fate. He had worked all night, splashing through the rainswept streets while hundreds of thousands of Parisians slept in their beds. The investigation was no longer his, since the Police Judiciaire had taken over, but he had still done his utmost, knowing others would take the glory, and he had come up with something.

He had been there for half an hour, waiting with a strange young man with long hair, pallid skin and pinched nostrils, who was staring straight ahead and looking as if he was about to pass out.

Naturally no one was paying any attention to him. They were just letting him stew. Nobody even asked him who his companion was or what he knew. Maigret simply muttered, 'In a minute, Lognon!'

He allowed the woman to go first, opened the door of his office and stepped aside:

'Would you be so kind as to take a seat?'

Maigret quickly realized he had been mistaken. Because of his conversation with Rose and the respectable, slightly stiff aspect of his visitor, her black clothes, her air of disdain, his first thought had been that she was Arlette's mother, who had recognized her daughter's photograph in the newspapers.

Her opening remark did not set him straight.

'I live in Lisieux and I took the first morning train.'

Lisieux is not far from the sea. As far as he could remember, there was a convent round there.

'I saw the newspaper yesterday evening and immediately recognized the photograph.'

She looked upset, thinking that was the appropriate expression to wear in the circumstances, but she wasn't sad at all. If anything, there was a glint of triumph in her little black eyes.

'Obviously in four years the girl's had time to change, and her hairstyle in particular makes her look different. Nonetheless I am certain that it's her. I would have gone to see my sister-in-law, but we haven't spoken for years, and it's not for me to make the first move. You understand?'

'I understand,' Maigret said gravely, taking a little drag on his pipe.

'The name isn't the same either, obviously. But it's normal, when people lead that life, for them to change their name. I was taken aback, though, to find out that she took the name Arlette and that she had an identity card in the name of Jeanne Leleu. The strangest thing is that I knew the Leleus . . .'

He waited patiently, watching the snow fall.

'In any case, I showed the photograph to three different people, reliable people who knew Anne-Marie well, and all three were positive. It's definitely her, my brother and sister-in-law's daughter.'

'Is your brother still alive?'

'He died when the child was only two. He was killed in a train accident which you may remember, the famous Rouen disaster. I'd told him . . .'

'Your sister-in-law lives in Lisieux?'

'She's never set foot out of the area. But, as I have said, we don't see each other. It would take too long to explain.

There are people in life, aren't there, who you just can't get along with. Say no more!'

'Say no more!' he repeated.

Then he asked:

'Incidentally, what's your brother's name?'

'Trochain. Gaston Trochain. We are a large family, probably the largest in Lisieux, and one of the oldest. I don't know if you know the area?'

'No, madame. I have only passed through.'

'Then in that case you've seen the statue of General Trochain on the square. He's our great-grandfather. And if you take the Caen road, the chateau you see on the right, with a slate-tiled roof, used to belong to the family. It's not ours any more. It was bought up after the 1914 war by some nouveaux riches. My brother still had a good job, though.'

'Is it indiscreet to ask what he did?'

'He was an inspector in the Forestry Commission. As for my sister-in-law, she's the daughter of an ironmonger who made a little money, so she inherited a dozen houses and two farms. When my brother was alive, we saw her for his sake. But as soon as she became a widow, everyone realized she was out of place, and now she is more or less always on her own in her big house.'

'You think she's read the article too?'

'Without a doubt. The photo was on the front page of the local paper that everyone gets.'

'Doesn't it surprise you that there hasn't been any word from her?'

'No, inspector. And I'm pretty sure there won't be. She is too proud for that. I'd even bet that if she were shown the body she'd swear it wasn't her daughter. I know she hasn't heard from her in four years. No one in Lisieux has. And it's not her daughter she's worried about, it's what people think of her.'

'Do you know under what circumstances the young girl came to leave her mother's house?'

'I tell you, no one could live with that woman. But there was something else. I don't know who the girl took after. It certainly wasn't my brother, everyone will tell you that. Be that as it may, when she was fifteen, she was expelled from her convent. After that, if I had to go out in the evening, I wouldn't dare look in a darkened doorway in case I saw her in there with a man. A married man, even. My sister-in-law thought she'd get the better of her by locking her in, which has never been a good approach, and that only made her wilder. In town they talk about how she once climbed out of the window without her shoes and was seen tramping the streets barefoot.'

'Does she have any distinctive features which would make you absolutely certain of recognizing her?'

'Yes, inspector.'

'What?'

'I have unfortunately not had children. My husband has never been very strong and he has been ill for years. When my niece was little, we hadn't fallen out yet, her mother and I. As the sister-in-law, I often looked after the baby of the family and I remember that she had a birthmark under her left heel, a little wine-coloured stain that never went.'

Maigret picked up the telephone and called the Forensic Institute.

'Hello, Police Judiciaire here. Will you examine the left foot of the young woman who was brought in yesterday? . . . Yes . . . I'll stay on the line . . . Tell me anything you notice in particular . . .'

She waited with absolute self-assurance, like a woman who has never been prone to self-doubt, sitting very upright in her chair, both hands propped on the silver clasp of her bag. You could imagine her sitting like that in church, listening to a sermon with the same hard, closed expression.

'Hello? Yes . . . That's all . . . Thank you . . . You're most likely going to have a visit from someone who will identify the body . . .'

He turned towards the woman from Lisieux.

'I assume you won't find that frightening?'

'It's my duty,' she answered.

He couldn't face keeping poor Lognon waiting any longer, let alone accompany his visitor to the morgue. He scanned the next-door office for someone.

'You free, Lucas?'

'I've just finished my report on the Javel business.'

'Could you take this lady to the morgue?'

She was taller than the sergeant and very wiry, and as she walked ahead of him down the corridor, it looked slightly as if she were leading him on a leash.

6.

When Lognon came in, pushing in front of him his prisoner, whose hair was so long that it bunched in a roll at the nape of his neck, Maigret noticed that the latter was carrying a heavy, brown canvas case, held together with string, which was making him walk lopsided.

Maigret opened a door and ushered the young man into the inspectors' office.

'See what's in there,' he told his men, pointing at the suitcase.

Then, as he was walking away, he had another thought.

'Get him to take down his trousers to see if he injects.'

Alone with Lognon, he observed the hard-done-by inspector benignly. He didn't begrudge him his ill-humour, knowing that his wife didn't help make his life a pleasant experience. He wasn't the only one of his colleagues who was perfectly willing to be agreeable to Lognon. But it was too much for them. The moment they saw his lugubrious face, always looking as if he sensed some impending doom, they couldn't help shrugging their shoulders or smiling.

At heart, Maigret suspected he enjoyed grumbling about his misfortune and had turned it into his personal vice, which he lovingly nurtured the way some old men nurture their chronic bronchitis to earn people's pity.

'Well, my friend?'

'Well, here we are.'

Which meant that Lognon was ready to answer any questions, since he was merely a low-ranking police officer, but that he thought it outrageous that his good self, to whom the investigation would have fallen if the Police Judiciaire hadn't existed, who knew his neighbourhood like the back of his hand and who hadn't allowed himself a minute's rest since the previous evening, should now have to account for himself.

The downturn of his mouth eloquently communicated:

'I know what's going to happen. It's always the way. You're going to worm everything I know out of me, and tomorrow – or soon, at any rate – the newspapers will announce that Detective Chief Inspector Maigret has solved the problem. Yet again they'll go on about his intuition, his methods.'

At heart, Lognon didn't believe a word of it, which probably explained his attitude. The fact that Maigret was a detective chief inspector, that other men in the building were in the special squad rather than kicking their heels outside a local police station, was simply because they had been lucky, or had friends in the right places, or knew how to sell themselves.

As far as he was concerned, no one had more to offer than Lognon.

'Where did you dig him up?'

'Gare du Nord.'

'When?'

'This morning, at six thirty. It was still dark.'

'You know his name?'

'I've known it for ages. This is the eighth time I've arrested him. We generally use his first name, Philippe. He's called Philippe Montemart, and his father is a professor at Nancy University.'

It was surprising hearing Lognon vouchsafing this much information in one go. His shoes were muddy and old and must have let in water; his trouser bottoms were soaked up to the knee; his eyes were tired and red-rimmed.

'You knew it was him the moment the concierge mentioned a young man with long hair?'

'I know this neighbourhood.'

Meaning, in a word, that Maigret and his men had no business getting involved.

'You went to his place? Where does he live?'

'In what used to be a maid's room in a building on Boulevard Rochechouart. He wasn't there.'

'What time was it?'

'Six o'clock, yesterday evening.'

'Had he taken his suitcase?'

'Not at that point.'

Lognon was the most tenacious bloodhound imaginable, you had to give him that. He had set off on a lead, with no way of knowing if it was the right one, and he had pursued it without faltering.

'You were looking for him from six o'clock yesterday evening until this morning?'

'I know the places he goes. He needed money to leave town and was doing the rounds looking for someone to scrounge off. It was only when he had got the money that he went and fetched his suitcase.'

'How did you know he was at the Gare du Nord?'

'A girl saw him take the first bus from Square d'Anvers. I found him in the waiting room.'

'And what have you been doing with him since seven this morning?'

'I took him to the station to question him.'

'And?'

'He won't say anything or doesn't know anything.'

It was strange. Maigret sensed the inspector was in a hurry to be off, and it probably wasn't because he wanted to go to bed.

'I suppose I'm leaving him with you?'

'Have you written your report?'

'I'll give it to my chief inspector this evening.'

'Did Philippe supply the countess with drugs?'

'Unless she gave them to him. At any rate, they were often seen together.'

'And had been for a long time?'

'A few months. If you don't need me any more . . .'

He definitely had a plan. Either Philippe had told him something that had set him thinking or else, while he was searching the previous night, he had gleaned the inkling of a lead and he was in a hurry to pursue it before anyone else could.

Maigret was familiar with the neighbourhood too and he could imagine the sort of night Philippe and the inspector had had. To drum up money, the young man would have had to try all his contacts and must have scoured the world of drug addicts. No doubt he had worked his way through all the girls touting for business outside sleazy hotels, the café waiters, the nightclub errand boys. Then, when the streets emptied out, he would have knocked at the door of a dump where other outcasts of his kind lived, just as pathetic and penniless as himself.

Had he at least got some drugs for himself? If not, he was going to keel over at any moment.

'Can I go?'

'Thank you. You've done good work.'

'I'm not saying he killed the old woman.'

'I'm not either.'

'Are you going to detain him?'

'Possibly.'

Lognon left, and Maigret opened the door to the inspectors' room. The suitcase lay open on the floor. Philippe, whose face was the colour and consistency of melted wax, lifted his arm every time someone moved, as if he were afraid of being hit.

No one in the room showed a flicker of sympathy, and the same expression of disgust could be read on every face.

The suitcase only contained shabby clothes, a spare pair of socks, some bottles of medicine – Maigret smelled them to check it wasn't heroin – and a number of notebooks.

He leafed through them. They were poems, or, more exactly, incoherent phrases generated by an addict's ravings.

'Come here!' he said.

Philippe inched past him like someone who expects a kick up the backside. It must have been a familiar occurrence. Even in Montmartre there are people who can't see someone of his sort without laying into him.

Maigret sat down without offering him a seat, and the young man remained standing, sniffing constantly, his nose dry, his nostrils twitching infuriatingly.

'The countess was your mistress?'

'She was my protector.'

He said these words in the voice and accent of a homosexual.

'Meaning you didn't sleep with her?'

'She took an interest in my writing.'

'And gave you money?'

'She helped me live.'

'Did she give you much?'

'She wasn't rich.'

For evidence, one only had to look at his well-cut but threadbare suit, a blue double-breasted affair. His shoes must have been a present as well, because they were patent leather and would have gone better with a dinner jacket than the dirty raincoat he had on.

'Why did you try to run away to Belgium?'

He didn't answer immediately, glancing at the neighbouring office's door as if he were afraid that Maigret was going to call in two brawny inspectors to give him a thrashing. Perhaps that had happened when he had been arrested before.

'I haven't done anything wrong. I don't understand why I've been arrested.'

'Do you like men?'

Deep down, like all fairies, he was proud of it, and an involuntary smile formed on his unnaturally red lips. Maybe getting told off by real men turned him on?

'You'd rather not answer?'

'I have men friends.'

'But you also have women friends?'

'It's not the same.'

'If I understand correctly, the men friends are for pleasure and the old ladies are for your daily bread?'

'They like my company.'

'Do you know many of them?'

'Three or four.'

'Are they all your protectors?'

It took considerable self-control for him to be able to speak about these things in an ordinary voice, to treat the youngster as a man like himself.

'They help me sometimes.'

'Do they all use drugs?'

When he turned his head away without replying, Maigret lost his temper. He didn't get to his feet, didn't grab him by the filthy collar of his raincoat and shake him, but his voice became quiet, his delivery staccato.

'Listen! I haven't got much patience today, and I'm not called Lognon. Either you start talking this minute or I'm going to stick you behind bars for a good long stretch. But not before I let my inspectors have it out with you.'

'You mean they'll hit me?'

'They'll do whatever they feel like doing.'

'They've no right to do that.'

'And you've no right to ruin the view. Now, try to answer my questions. How long have you known the countess?'

'About six months.'

'Where did you meet her?'

'In a little bar on Rue Victor-Massé, practically opposite her apartment.'

'You realized straight away that she shot up?'

'It was easy to tell.'

'Did you turn on the charm?'

'I asked her to give me a little.'

'She had some?'

'Yes.'

'A lot?'

'She almost never ran out.'

'Do you know how she got it?'

'She didn't tell me.'

'Answer the question. Do you know?'

'I think so.'

'How?'

'From a doctor.'

'A doctor who takes it too?'

'Yes.'

'Doctor Bloch?'

'I don't know his name.'

'You're lying. Did you go and see him?'

'Sometimes.'

'Why?'

'So he'd give me some.'

'Did he?'

'Once.'

'Because you threatened to talk?'

'I was desperate. I hadn't had any for three days. He gave me an injection, just one.'

'Where did you meet up with the countess?'

'In the bar and at her apartment.'

'Why did she give you morphine and money?'

'Because she took an interest in me.'

'I've told you, you'd better answer my questions.'

'She felt lonely.'

'Didn't she know anyone?'

'She was always on her own.'

'Did you make love?'

'I tried to please her.'

'At her apartment?'

'Yes.'

'And you both drank red wine?'

'It made me ill.'

'And then you'd fall asleep on her bed. Did you sometimes spend the night?'

'I sometimes stayed a couple of days.'

'Without opening the curtains, I'm sure. Without knowing when it was day and when it was night. Is that right?'

Then he must have roamed the streets like a sleepwalker, in a world he no longer belonged to, looking for someone else with drugs.

'How old are you?'

'Twenty-eight.'

'When did you start?'

'Three or four years ago.'

'Why?'

'I don't know.'

'Are you still in touch with your parents?'

'My father wished me in hell a long time ago.'

'And your mother?'

'She secretly sends me a postal order every so often.'

'Tell me about the countess.'

'I don't know anything.'

'Say what you know.'

'She used to be very rich. She was married to a man she didn't love, an old man who wouldn't let her alone for a minute and had her followed by a private detective.'

'Is that what she told you?'

'Yes. Every day he got a report saying what she had been doing, almost by the minute.'

'Was she already injecting then?'

'No. I don't think so. He died and everyone was hellbent on getting their hands on the money he left her.'

'Who's everyone?'

'Every gigolo on the Côte d'Azur, the professional gamblers, her girlfriends . . .'

'She never mentioned any names?'

'I don't remember any. You know how it is. When you've had your fix, talking's different.'

Maigret only knew from hearsay, never having tried it himself.

'Did she still have money?'

'Not much. I think she was selling her jewellery as she went along.'

'Did you see it?'

'No.'

'Was she suspicious of you?'

'I don't know.'

He was so unsteady on his legs, which must have been skeletal under his baggy trousers, that Maigret motioned to him to sit down.

'Was there anyone in Paris, besides you, who was still trying to squeeze her for money?'

'She didn't mention anyone.'

'You never saw anyone in her apartment, or with her in the street, or in a bar?'

Maigret sensed a definite hesitation.

'N . . . no.'

He gave him a hard look.

'You haven't forgotten what I told you?'

But Philippe had gathered his wits.

'I never saw anyone with her.'

'Man or woman?'

'No one.'

'You didn't hear any mention of the name Oscar either?'

'I don't know anyone called that.'

'She never seemed afraid of anyone?'

'All she was afraid of was dying alone.'

'She never argued with you?'

He was too pale to blush, but there was still a vague colouring of the tips of his ears.

'How do you know that?'

With a knowing, slightly contemptuous smile, he added:

'It always ended that way.'

'Explain.'

'Ask anyone.'

Meaning: 'Anyone who takes drugs.'

Then, dully, as if he knew he wouldn't be understood:

'When she ran out and couldn't get any immediately, she would fly into a rage with me, accusing me of begging her for morphine, even of stealing it, and swear there had been six or twelve phials in the drawer the day before.'

'You had a key to her apartment?'

'No.'

'You never went in when she wasn't there?'

'She was almost always there. Sometimes she'd go a week or more without leaving her bedroom.'

'Answer my question yes or no. You never went into her apartment when she wasn't there?'

A hesitation again, barely noticeable.

'No.'

Maigret muttered as if to himself, without pressing the point:

'You're lying!'

Thanks to this Philippe character, the atmosphere in his office had become almost as suffocating and unreal as that of the apartment on Rue Victor-Massé.

Maigret had enough knowledge of drug addicts to know that there must have been occasions, when he had run out, that Philippe would have been driven to get some at any price. Like the night before, when he was trying to scrape enough money together to leave, an addict would go around every single person he knew at times like that and put his hand out without a shred of human respect.

At the bottom of the heap, where the young man spent his days, that couldn't always be easy. So how could it fail to occur to him that the countess almost always had morphine in her drawer and that, if she was being tight-fisted with it, he just had to wait until she went out?

It was only a hunch, but entirely logical.

These people watched each other's every move. Racked with jealousy, they stole from, and sometimes informed on, one another. The Police Judiciaire had lost count of the number of anonymous telephone calls from addicts wanting revenge.

'When did you see her for the last time?'

'The day before yesterday, in the morning.'

'You're sure it wasn't yesterday morning?'

'Yesterday morning I was sick and didn't get out of bed.'

'What was wrong?'

'I hadn't found any for two days.'

'She didn't give you any?'

'She swore she'd run out and that the doctor hadn't been able to give her some.'

'Did you argue?'

'We were both in a bad mood.'

'Did you believe her?'

'She showed me the empty drawer.'

'When was she expecting the doctor?'

'She didn't know. She'd rung him, and he'd promised to go and see her.'

'You didn't go back to her apartment?'

'No.'

'Right, listen carefully. The countess's body was found yesterday around five p.m. The evening papers were already out. So the news only ran this morning. But you spent all night looking for money to go to Belgium. How did you know the countess was dead?'

He was visibly on the verge of replying: 'I didn't know.'

Maigret's hard stare, however, made him change his mind.

'I was passing her building and I saw a crowd on the pavement.'

'What time?'

'About six thirty.'

That had been when Maigret was in the apartment and a policeman had in fact been keeping gawkers away from the door.

'Empty your pockets.'

'Inspector Lognon has already made me empty them.'

'Do it again.'

He took out a dirty handkerchief, two keys on a key ring – one was the key of the suitcase – a penknife, a purse, a little tin containing pills, a wallet, a notebook and a hypodermic syringe in its case. Maigret seized the notebook, which was already old, its pages yellowed. It contained a mass of addresses and telephone numbers: almost no surnames, just initials or first names. Oscar was not one of them.

'When you found out that the countess had been strangled, did you think you would be suspected?'

'That's always the way.'

'So you decided to go to Belgium? You know someone there?'

'I've been to Brussels a few times.'

'Who gave you the money?'

'A friend.'

'Which friend?'

'I don't know his name.'

'You'd better tell me.'

'It was the doctor.'

'Doctor Bloch?'

'Yes. I hadn't had any luck. It was three in the morning, and I was getting scared. I ended up calling him from a bar on Rue Caulaincourt.'

'What did you say to him?'

'That I was a friend of the countess and that I needed money very badly.'

'Did it work immediately?'

'I added that if I was arrested he could have some problems.'

'In a word, you blackmailed him. He told you to meet him at his surgery?'

'He told me to go to Rue Victor-Massé, where he lives, and said he'd be on the pavement.'

'You didn't ask him for anything else?'

'He gave me a phial.'

'I suppose you shot it up immediately in some doorway? Is that it? Got everything off your chest now?'

'That's all I know.'

'Is the doctor a fairy too?'

'No.'

'How do you know?'

Philippe shrugged, as if the question were too naive.

'Are you hungry?'

'No.'

'Thirsty?'

The young man's lips were trembling, but food and drink were not what he needed.

Maigret got up as if it was an effort and opened the connecting door once again. Torrence happened to be there, big and strong, with his butcher's apprentice's hands. The people he interrogated were far from suspecting how softhearted he really was.

'Come here,' Maigret said to him. 'You're going to shut yourself up with this lad and only let him go when he's coughed up everything he knows. Doesn't matter whether it takes twenty-four hours or three days. When you're tired, get someone to relieve you.'

Philippe protested, wild-eyed:

'I've told you all I know. You're taking advantage of me.'

Then, raising his voice like an angry woman:

'You're a brute! . . . You're mean! . . . You . . . you . . .'

Standing aside to let him past, Maigret exchanged winks with the hefty Torrence. The men crossed the large inspectors' office and went into a room jokingly known as the chamber of confessions, although not before Torrence had called to Lapointe, 'Get some beer and sandwiches sent up!'

Once alone with his subordinates, Maigret stretched and sneezed and very nearly went and opened the window.

'Well, then, boys?'

Only then did he notice that Lucas was back already.

'She's here again, chief, waiting to talk to you.'

'The aunt from Lisieux? Incidentally, how did she react?'

'Like an old woman who loves other people's funerals. No need for vinegar or smelling salts there. She coldly examined the body from head to toe. In the middle of her examination she gave a start, then asked, "Why have they shaved her?" I told her it wasn't us, and she was stunned. She pointed out the birthmark on the sole of her foot. "You see! Even without that I'd still recognize her." Then, as she was leaving, without asking my opinion, she announced, "I'm coming back with you. I have to talk to the detective chief inspector." She's in the outer room. I don't think it's going to be that easy getting rid of her.'

Young Lapointe had just picked up the telephone and seemed to have a bad connection.

'Is that Nice?' Maigret asked.

Lapointe nodded. Janvier wasn't there. Maigret went back into his office and rang for the clerk to show in the old lady from Lisieux.

'Apparently you've got something to say to me?'

'I don't know if you'll be interested. I've been thinking as I went along. You know how it is. You can't help but go over memories. Not that I'd want people to think me a gossip.'

'I'm listening.'

'It's about Anne-Marie. I told you this morning that she left Lisieux four years ago and that her mother never once tried to find out what had become of her, which, between ourselves, strikes me as a monstrous way for a mother to behave.'

He just had to wait. It would be pointless hurrying her.

'People talked about it a great deal, naturally. Lisieux is a little town where everything comes out in the wash eventually. Well, a woman whom I trust implicitly and goes to Caen every week, where she has a share in a business, swore to me on her husband's life that, not long after Anne-Marie left, she bumped into her in Caen just as the young girl was going into a doctor's.'

She paused with a self-satisfied air, but, to her surprise, Maigret didn't ask her anything. With a sigh, she went on, 'Well, it wasn't just any old doctor, it was Doctor Potut, the obstetrician.'

'In other words, you suspect your niece left town because she was pregnant?'

'That's the rumour that went round, and people asked themselves who the father might be.'

'Did they find out?'

'They named names, and they were nothing if not spoiled for choice. But I always had my own pet theory, and that's why I've come back to see you. It's my duty to help you discover the truth, isn't it?'

She was beginning to think the police were not as inquiring as they were made out to be, because Maigret wasn't assisting her at all. He wasn't urging her to speak, but listening as indifferently as an old confessor dozing behind his screen.

She declared, as if it was of the utmost importance:

'Anne-Marie always had a weak throat. She'd get a sore throat once every winter, if not more, and it didn't get any better when she had her tonsils out. That year, I remember, my sister-in-law had the idea of taking her for a rest cure to La Bourbole, where they specialize in treating throat ailments.'

Maigret remembered Arlette's slightly hoarse voice, which he had put down to drinking, cigarettes and sleepless nights.

'When she left Lisieux, her condition wasn't showing yet, which suggests that she can't have been more than three or four months pregnant. At the very most. Because she was still wearing very tight dresses. Well, that fits exactly with her stay at La Bourbole. I'd swear she met a man there who got her pregnant, and then she probably went off to be with him. If it had been someone from Lisieux, he would have got her to have an abortion or left town with her.'

Maigret slowly lit his pipe. He felt aching and stiff, as if he'd walked a long way, but it was just nausea. As he had when Philippe was there, he would have liked to go over and open the window.

'I suppose you're going back?'

'Not today. I'll probably stay on a few days in Paris. I have some friends I can stay with. I'll leave you their address.'

It was near Boulevard Pasteur. The address was already filled out on the back of one of her visiting cards, complete with a telephone number.

'You can call me if you need me.'

'Thank you.'

'I am entirely at your service.'

'I have no doubt you are.'

He led her back to the door without a smile, closed it slowly behind her, stretched and scratched his head with both hands, sighing quietly:

'What a filthy bunch!'

'Can I come in, chief?'

It was Lapointe, who was holding a sheet of paper in his hand and seemed very excited.

'Did you ring for some beer?'

'The waiter from the Brasserie Dauphine has just brought up the tray.'

It hadn't been taken into Torrence's box room yet, and Maigret took the cool, foaming glass and drained it in one long draught.

'Just have to call and tell them to bring another!'

7.

'First I have to pass on young Julien's respects and affection,' Lapointe said, not without a hint of jealousy. 'Apparently you'll understand.'

'Is he in Nice?'

'He was transferred there from Limoges a few weeks ago.'

He was the son of an old inspector who had worked with Maigret and retired to the Côte d'Azur. As it transpired, Maigret hadn't seen young Julien pretty much since the days when he used to dandle him on his knee.

'He's who I rang yesterday evening,' went on Lapointe, 'and I've been in touch with him ever since. When he knew I was ringing on your behalf, the prospect of working for you seemed to energize him, and he was falling over backwards to help. He has spent hours in an attic in the police station, turning their old archives upside down. Apparently there's a mass of bundles of paper tied up with string, case reports that everyone's forgotten. They're all jumbled together in a pile that almost reaches to the ceiling.'

'Did he find the file for the Farnheim case?'

'He's just telephoned me with the list of witnesses who were interviewed after the count's death. I especially asked him to get me the one of the servants who worked at The Oasis. I'll read it to you:

> Antoinette Méjat, nineteen, maid.
> Rosalie Moncœur, forty-two, cook.
> Maria Pinaco, twenty-three, kitchen maid.
> Angelino Luppin, thirty-eight, butler.

Maigret waited, standing near the window of his office and watching the snow, which was beginning to thin out. Lapointe paused in an actorly way:

'Oscar Bonvoisin, thirty-five, valet-chauffeur.'

'An Oscar!' said Maigret. 'I suppose we don't know what's become of these people?'

'Well, Inspector Julien had an idea. He hasn't been in Nice for long, and he's been struck by the number of wealthy foreigners who move there for a few months, rent largish houses and live in grand style. He thought to himself that they must have to find staff pretty much overnight. And, sure enough, he's found an employment agency that specializes in domestic staff for big houses. It's been run by the same old lady for over twenty years. She doesn't remember Count von Farnheim or the countess. She doesn't remember Oscar Bonvoisin either, but barely a year ago she found a position for the cook, who is one of her regulars. Rosalie Moncœur these days works for some South Americans who have a villa in Nice and spend part of the year in Paris. I've got their address: 132 Avenue d'Iéna. According to this lady, they should be in Paris now.'

'Do we know anything about the others?'

'Julien is still looking into it. Do you want me to go and see her, chief?'

Maigret nearly said yes to please Lapointe, who was dying to question the Farnheims' former cook.

'I'll go myself,' he decided eventually.

Primarily, if he was honest, this was because he wanted to get some fresh air, have another glass of beer and generally escape the atmosphere in his office, which he had found stifling all morning.

'While I'm gone, go and check in Records that there's nothing under Bonvoisin. You'll need to check with the Hotel Agency too. Ring round the town halls and police stations.'

'Fine, chief.'

Poor Lapointe! Maigret felt remorse, but he wasn't in any mood to give up his walk.

Before leaving, he opened the door of the box room, where Torrence and Philippe were shut away. The heavy-set Torrence had taken off his jacket, but his forehead was still beaded with sweat. Perched on the edge of his chair, white as a sheet, Philippe looked as if he was about to faint.

Maigret didn't need to ask any questions. He knew Torrence wouldn't give up and was prepared to keep going until it got dark, and all night if need be.

Less than half an hour later, his taxi stopped in front of a sombre building on the Avenue d'Iéna, and a male concierge in a dark uniform greeted Maigret in a hall with marble columns.

Maigret said who he was, asked if Rosalie Moncœur still worked in the building and was shown to the backstairs.

'Third floor.'

He had drunk two more glasses of beer on the way, so his headache had gone. It was a narrow spiral staircase, and he counted the floors under his breath. He rang at a brown door. A stout woman with white hair opened it and looked at him in astonishment.

'Madame Moncœur?'

'What do you want with her?'

'To talk to her.'

'It's me.'

She was watching her stoves while a dark-skinned young girl was running an aromatic mixture through a food mill.

'You worked for the Count and Countess von Farnheim, if I am not mistaken?'

'Who are you?'

'Police Judiciaire.'

'You're not going to tell me you're digging up that old story?'

'Not exactly. Have you heard that the countess is dead?'

'Happens to everyone. But no, I didn't know that.'

'It was in the papers this morning.'

'Do you think I read the papers? With bosses who give dinners for fifteen to twenty people almost every day?'

'She was murdered.'

'That's funny.'

'Why do you think it's funny?'

She did not offer him a chair and carried on working, talking to him as she would a supplier. She was obviously a woman who had been through hard times, not easily impressed.

'I don't know why I said that. Who killed her?'

'We don't know yet, that's what I'm trying to establish. You continued working for her after her husband's death?'

'Only for two weeks. We did not get along.'

'Why?'

While keeping an eye on what the girl was doing, she opened the oven to baste a piece of chicken.

'Because it wasn't the job for me.'

'You mean it wasn't a respectable household?'

'If you like. I am fond of my work and want people to sit down to eat on time and know roughly what they're eating. That's enough, Irma. Get the hardboiled eggs out of the fridge and separate the yolks from the whites.'

She opened a bottle of Madeira and poured a long slug into a sauce, which she stirred slowly with a wooden spoon.

'Do you remember Oscar Bonvoisin?'

She gave him a look, as if to say, 'So that's what you were driving at!'

But she didn't say anything.

'Did you hear my question?'

'I'm not deaf.'

'What kind of man was he?'

'A valet.'

He was surprised by her tone, and she added:

'I don't like valets. They're all layabouts. Especially if they're chauffeurs too. They think no one in the house exists except for them and carry on worse than the bosses.'

'Was that the case with Bonvoisin?'

'I don't remember his last name. We always called him Oscar.'

'What was he like?'

'Good-looking, and he knew it. Well, there are some people who like that sort. I'm not one of them, and I told him so straight to his face.'

'Did he run after you?'

'In his way.'

'Meaning?'

'Why are you asking me all this?'

'Because I need to know.'

'You think he might have killed the countess?'

'It's possible.'

Of the three of them, Irma was the most transfixed by their conversation. She was so alarmed to be at one remove from a real crime that she did not know what she was doing any more.

'Well? Have you forgotten you've got to mash the yolks?'

'Can you describe him physically to me?'

'As he was then, yes. But I don't know what he's like now.'

As she said that there was a glint in her eye, which Maigret noticed.

'Are you sure?' he insisted. 'You've never seen him since?'

'That's just what I'm thinking. I'm not certain. A few weeks ago, I went to see my brother who runs a little café and I saw a man in the street who I thought I recognized. He was looking at me closely too, as if he was trying to remember something. Then I suddenly had the feeling he started walking very fast and looking the other way.'

'You thought it was Oscar?'

'Not immediately. It vaguely occurred to me afterwards, and now I would almost swear it was him.'

'Where is your brother's café?'

'Rue Caulaincourt.'

'You thought you recognized the former valet on a street in Montmartre?'

'Just around the corner from Place Clichy.'

'Now, try to tell me what sort of man he was.'

'I don't like snitching.'

'You'd rather let a murderer go free?'

'If he's only killed the countess, he hasn't done any great harm.'

'If he killed her, he's killed at least one other woman, and there's nothing to say he'll stop there.'

She shrugged.

'It's his bad luck then, isn't it? He wasn't tall. Short, if anything. And that annoyed him so much he'd wear high heels like a woman to make himself taller. I used to tease him about it, and he'd give me a filthy look, without saying a word.'

'Did he talk much?'

'He was very taciturn, never said what he was doing or what he was thinking. He was very dark-skinned, with thick, wiry hair and a low forehead, and he had thick black eyebrows. Some women thought they made his eyes irresistible. I didn't. He'd stare at you in a self-satisfied way, as if he thought he was the only person in the world and you were just a piece of shit. Sorry.'

'Don't mention it. Go on.'

Now she had started, she didn't hold back. She was on the move constantly in that kitchen full of delicious smells, juggling pots and utensils, occasionally darting the odd glance at the electric clock.

'He had his way with Antoinette, and she was crazy about him. Maria too.'

'You mean the maid and the kitchen maid?'

'Yes. And there were others, who passed through the house before them. It was the sort of place where the servants didn't stay long. You never knew if the old man or the countess was in charge. You know what I mean? Oscar didn't run after them, to use your expression just now. As soon as he clapped eyes on a new servant, he just looked at her as if he was taking possession of her. Then, the first night, he'd go upstairs and march into her room as if everything had been agreed. You get other men like him, who think we can't resist them. Antoinette shed her share of tears.'

'Why?'

'Because she was really in love with him and for a while she hoped he would marry her. But once he'd had his way with a girl, he'd leave without saying anything. Next day, he wouldn't take any notice of them. Never a kind word. Never a nice gesture. Until he'd get the urge again and he'd be back upstairs knocking on their door. It didn't stop him getting whatever he wanted, though, and not just with the servants.'

'You think he slept with the lady of the house?'

'Not more than two days after the count died.'

'How do you know?'

'Because I saw him coming out of her room at six in the morning. That's one of the reasons I left. When the servants start sharing their bosses' beds, it's all over.'

'Did he act like the master of the house?'

'He did whatever he wanted. It was as though no one could give him orders any more.'

'It never occurred to you that the count might have been murdered?'

'It was none of my business.'

'But did you think it?'

'Didn't the police too? Why else would they have questioned us?'

'Could it have been Oscar?'

'I didn't say that. She was probably just as capable of it as he was.'

'You continued working in Nice?'

'In Nice and Monte-Carlo. I like the climate in the south, and it's only by chance that I followed my bosses to Paris and I'm here now.'

'You haven't heard of the countess since?'

'I've seen her round and about once or twice, but we don't go to the same places.'

'And Oscar?'

'I never saw him in the south again. I don't think he stayed on the Côte.'

'But you think you spotted him a few weeks ago. Describe him to me.'

'You can tell you're in the police. You think that when you meet someone in the street, you've got nothing better to do than make a note of their description.'

'Has he aged?'

'As much as I have. He's fifteen years older.'

'Which makes him in his fifties.'

'I'm almost ten years older than him. Another three or four years working for other people and I'm retiring to a small house that I've bought in Cagnes, where the only cooking I'll do is what I'm going to eat. Fried eggs and chops.'

'Do you remember how he was dressed?'

'On Place Clichy?'

'Yes.'

'He was in pretty dark clothes. I wouldn't say black, but dark, definitely. He was wearing a big overcoat and gloves. I noticed the gloves. He was very smart.'

'His hair?'

'He wasn't walking around in winter with his hat in his hand.'

'Was he greying at the temples?'

'I think so. But that's not what struck me.'

'What did?'

'That he'd put on weight. He was broad-shouldered as he was before. He used to make a point of walking around bare-chested because he was incredibly muscular, and that impressed the women. You wouldn't have thought he was that strong, if you saw him when he was dressed. Nowadays, if he's who I ran into, he looks a bit like a bull. His neck has thickened, and he seems even shorter.'

'Have you heard from Antoinette?'

'She died. Not long afterwards.'

'Of what?'

'A miscarriage. At least that's what I was told.'

'And Maria Pinaco?'

'I don't know if she's still going: the last time I saw her, she was on the game, working on Cours Albert-Premier, in Nice.'

'Was that long ago?'

'Two years. Maybe a bit more.'

She was curious enough to ask:

'How was the countess killed?'

'Strangled.'

She didn't say anything, but seemed not to think that was too out of keeping with Oscar's character.

'And who's the other one?'

'A girl you won't have known; she was only twenty.'

'Thanks for reminding me that I'm an old woman.'

'I didn't mean that. She's from Lisieux, and there's nothing to suggest that she ever lived in the south. All I know is that she went to La Bourboule.'

'Near Le Mont-Dore?'

'In the Auvergne, yes.'

She suddenly looked at Maigret with a thoughtful expression.

'I've started snitching, so I guess . . .' she muttered. 'Oscar was from the Auvergne. I don't know exactly where, but he had a bit of an accent, and when I wanted to rile him, I'd call him a charcoal-seller. He'd go deathly pale. Now, if you don't mind, I'd rather you made yourself scarce, because my people are sitting down to eat in half an hour, and I need my kitchen to myself.'

'I may come back and see you again.'

'As long as you're only as unpleasant as you were today! What's your name?'

'Maigret.'

He saw the girl, who must read the papers, give a start, but the cook had clearly never heard of him.

'Easy name to remember. Especially because you're on the fat side. Actually, to finish off about Oscar, he's roughly as big as you nowadays, but shorter by a head. Can you picture that?'

'Thank you.'

'Not at all. One thing, though: if you do arrest him, I'd just as soon not be called as a witness. Bosses never like it. And lawyers ask you loads of questions to try to make you look stupid. I did it once and I swore I'd never fall for that trick again. So don't count on me.'

She closed the door quietly behind him, and Maigret had to walk the length of the avenue before he found a taxi. Instead of getting it to take him to Quai des Orfèvres, he went home for lunch. He got to the Police Judiciaire around 2.30, by which point the snow had stopped completely and the streets were covered with a thin layer of slippery, blackish mud.

When he opened the door of the box room, it was blue with smoke, and there were twenty or so cigarettes in the ashtray. Torrence had smoked them all because Philippe was not a smoker. There was a tray with the remains of some sandwiches and five empty beer glasses.

'Will you come here for a moment?'

Once they were in the next-door office, Torrence mopped his brow and relaxed, sighing:

'He's exhausting, that guy. He's as limp as a rag doll, there's nothing to get hold of. Twice I thought he's going to talk. I'm sure he's got something to say. His resistance seemed shot. His eyes begged for mercy. Then at the last second, he changes his mind and swears he doesn't know anything. It makes me sick. Just now, he drove me so crazy I smacked him full in the face. Do you know what he did?'

Maigret didn't say anything.

'He held his cheek and started whining as if he was talking to another fairy like him, "You're mean!" I mustn't do it again, I bet it excites him.'

Maigret could not help smiling.

'Shall I keep at it?'

'Have another go. Maybe we'll try something else in a minute. Has he had anything to eat?'

'He picked half-heartedly at a sandwich with his pinkie in the air. You can tell he's missing the morphine. If I promised to give him some maybe he'd talk. The Drug Squad must have some, don't they?'

'I'll talk to the chief. But don't say anything for now. Just keep hammering away at him.'

Torrence looked around at the familiar setting, took a deep breath and then plunged back into the depressing atmosphere of the box room.

'Any news, Lapointe?'

Lapointe had been on the telephone virtually all morning, making do with a sandwich and a glass of beer like Torrence.

'A dozen Bonvoisins, but no Oscar Bonvoisin.'

'Try to get La Bourboule on the telephone. You might have more luck there.'

'Have you had a tip-off?'

'Maybe.'

'The cook?'

'She thinks she ran into him in Paris recently and, more interestingly, she says it was in Montmartre.'

'Why La Bourboule?'

'First because he is from the Auvergne, and secondly because Arlette apparently had a significant encounter there five years ago.'

Maigret wasn't too convinced.

'No news from Lognon?'

He telephoned the station on Rue de La Rochefoucauld himself, but Inspector Lognon had only dropped by for a second.

'He said he was working for you and would be out all day.'

Maigret spent a quarter of an hour pacing up and down his office, smoking his pipe. Then he seemed to come to a decision and headed for the commissioner's office.

'What's the latest, Maigret? You weren't at the briefing this morning.'

'I was asleep,' he admitted right out.

'Have you seen the afternoon papers?'

He made a dismissive gesture.

'They're wondering if there's going to be other women strangled.'

'I don't think so.'

'Why?'

'Because the countess and Arlette weren't killed by a maniac. Anything but: it was a man who knew exactly what he was doing.'

'Have you discovered his identity?'

'Perhaps. Probably.'

'Do you expect to arrest him today?'

'We'd need to know where he sleeps at night, and I haven't the slightest idea. It's most likely somewhere in Montmartre. There is only one scenario where there could be another victim.'

'Namely?'

'If Arlette talked to anyone else. If she confided in one of her girlfriends at Picratt's, Betty or Tania, for instance.'

'You've questioned them?'

'They're not saying anything. The owner, Fred, isn't saying anything. The Grasshopper isn't saying anything. And that nasty little worm Philippe isn't saying anything either, despite being under interrogation since this morning. He knows something, that fellow, I'd swear to it. He saw the countess regularly. She kept him supplied with morphine.'

'Where did she get it?'

'From her doctor.'

'Have you arrested him?'

'Not yet. That's the Drug Squad's affair. I've been wondering for the last hour whether I should risk something or not.'

'What's at stake?'

'Us having another dead body on our hands. That's what I want to ask your advice about. I'm sure that by going about things in the ordinary way, we'll end up getting our hands on this Bonvoisin character, who is most likely the two women's murderer. But it could take days or weeks. It'll be luck more than anything else. And, unless I am very mistaken, he's a sly one. Until we have him in handcuffs, he could kill someone, or a number of people, who know too much.'

'What's the risk you want to take?'

'I didn't say I wanted to.'

The commissioner smiled.

'Explain.'

'If Philippe knows something, as I'm convinced he does, Oscar must be worried at the moment. I just have to tell the newspapers that Philippe was interrogated for several hours to no effect and then release him.'

'I'm beginning to understand.'

'One possibility is that Philippe will rush to Oscar's house, but I'm not banking on that. Unless it's the only way for him to get the drugs he is starting to need desperately badly.'

'The other possibility?'

The chief had already guessed.

'Exactly. You can't trust an addict. Philippe hasn't talked, but that does not mean he'll hold his tongue for ever, Oscar knows that.'

'So he'll try to silence him.'

'Exactly! I didn't want to try it without talking it over with you.'

'You think you can stop him being killed?'

'I'll take every precaution. Bonvoisin is not the sort to use a gun. It makes too much noise, and he doesn't seem to like noise.'

'When do you plan on releasing the witness?'

'Early evening. It will be easier to tail him discreetly then. I will put as many men on him as it takes. And if there is an accident, well, I don't think it will be such a great loss.'

'I'd rather there wasn't.'

'Me too.'

Neither of them spoke for a while. Finally the commissioner merely sighed:

'It's your case, Maigret. Good luck.'

'You were right, chief.'

'Let's have it!'

Lapointe was so pleased to be playing an important role in an investigation that he had almost forgotten about Arlette's death.

'I got the information immediately. Oscar Bonvoisin was born in Le Mont-Dore, where his father was a hotel porter and his mother a chambermaid at the same place. He started off as a messenger boy himself. Then he moved away and didn't go back until about ten years ago, when he bought a villa, not in Le Mont-Dore but very near, in La Bourboule.'

'Does he live there?'

'No. He spends part of the summer there and the odd day in winter.'

'He's not married?'

'Confirmed bachelor. His mother's still alive.'

'Living in her son's villa?'

'No. She has a small apartment in town. People think he pays the bills. They say that he's earned a fair bit of money and has got a cushy job in Paris.'

'The description?'

'Fits.'

'Do you want to be given a vital job?'

'You know I do, chief.'

'Even if it's on the dangerous side, with a great deal of responsibility?'

His love for Arlette must have surged through his veins again, because he declared, a little too fervently:

'I don't care if I'm killed.'

'Good! That's not it, though. You'll be making sure someone else isn't. And for that it's essential that you don't look like a policeman.'

'Do you think I do?'

'Go to the cloakroom. Choose the clothes of a hardened shirker who's looking for a job and hoping he won't find one. Wear a cap instead of a hat. Don't overdo it, that's the main thing.'

Janvier had returned, and he gave him broadly similar instructions.

'People should think you're a clerk on his way home from work.'

Then he chose two inspectors whom Philippe had not seen before.

He called all four of them into his office and, standing in front of a map of Montmartre, explained what he wanted from them.

Night was falling fast. The lights on the embankment and Boulevard Saint-Michel were already on.

Maigret thought about waiting for it to be completely dark, but it would be harder to follow Philippe through the deserted streets without arousing his, and especially Bonvoisin's, suspicions.

'Do you want to come here for a moment, Torrence?'

The latter burst out:

'I give up! That fellow makes me sick. Someone else can have a go if he's got a strong stomach, but I'm . . .'

'You'll be done in five minutes.'

'Are we letting him go?'

'As soon as the fifth edition of the papers is out.'

'What have the newspapers got to do with it?'

'They're going to report that he has been questioned for hours with no joy.'

'Got it.'

'Shake him up a bit more. Then put his hat on his head and boot him out, saying he'd better watch his step.'

'Do I give him back his syringe?'

'His syringe and money.'

Torrence looked at the four inspectors who were waiting.

'Is that why they're in carnival get-up?'

One of the men hailed a taxi and waited in it near the entrance. Others went to take up their positions at strategic points.

Maigret had had time to ring the Drug Squad and the Rue de La Rochefoucauld station.

Through the door of the box room, which he had intentionally left ajar, Torrence's thunderous voice could be heard. He was throwing himself wholeheartedly into his part, telling Philippe to his face everything he thought of him.

'I wouldn't touch you with a bargepole, understand? I'd be too afraid you'd come. I'm going to have to get the office disinfected, as it is. Take this joke of an overcoat, put your hat on.'

'You mean I can go?'

'I'm telling you I've seen enough of you, we've all seen enough of you. We're sick of you, get it? Pick up your junk and disappear, you piece of shit!'

'There's no need to push me about.'

'I'm not pushing you about.'

'You're shouting at me.'

'Get out of here!'

'I'm going . . . I'm going . . . Thank you.'

A door was opened, then fiercely slammed shut. The corridor was deserted, with only two or three people waiting in the dimly lit waiting room.

Philippe's silhouette stood out against the long, dusty vista; he looked like an insect searching for a way out.

Maigret, who was watching him through his half-open door, finally saw him start down the stairs.

His heart sank a little. He closed the door and turned to Torrence, who was unwinding like an actor in his dressing room after the show. Torrence could see he was concerned, worried.

'You think he's going to get killed?'

'I hope someone will try but won't succeed.'

'His first priority will be to tear off to wherever he thinks he can get drugs.'

'That's right.'

'Do you know where that is?'

'Doctor Bloch's.'

'Will he give him any?'

'I've sent orders that he mustn't, and he won't dare disobey me.'

'So what now?'

'I don't know. I'm going up to Montmartre. The boys know where to reach me. You stay here. If there's anything, ring me at Picratt's.'

'In other words, more sandwiches for me. Doesn't matter. As long as it's not just me and that fairy!'

Maigret put on his overcoat and hat, chose two cold pipes from his desk and stuffed them into his pockets.

Before getting a taxi to take him to Rue Pigalle, he stopped at the Brasserie Dauphine and drank a glass of brandy. His hangover had cleared up, but he sensed that there would be another one along in the morning.

8.

The photographs of Arlette had finally been removed from the display. She had been replaced by another girl, who was presumably doing the same act, and maybe even wearing the same dress, but Betty was right: it was difficult to carry off. The girl may have been young and chubby, and pretty, really, but even in the photograph, as she undressed, there was something crudely vulgar about her which reminded you of dirty postcards and, a little, of those badly painted nudes you see rippling on the backcloths of fairground booths.

Maigret only had to push open the door. A light was on at the bar and another at the back of the room, with a long belt of half-darkness between the two.

Their apartment was so tiny that the Alfonsi had to use the club as a dining and sitting room during the day. No doubt, at aperitif time, customers who were more like friends would sometimes come to have a drink at the bar. Fred looked over his glasses as Maigret came towards him. He didn't stand up but offered him a big paw and gestured to him to sit down.

'I thought you'd show up,' he said.

He didn't explain why. Maigret didn't ask him. Fred finished reading the report about the inquiry in progress, took off his glasses and asked, 'What can I get you? A brandy?'

He went and filled two glasses and sat back down with the satisfied sigh of a man pleased to be at home. Both of them heard footsteps overhead.

'Is your wife up there?' asked Maigret.

'She's giving the new girl a lesson.'

Maigret didn't relish the thought of the heavyset Rose giving the young girl a striptease demonstration.

'You're not interested?' he asked Fred.

The latter shrugged his shoulders.

'She's a pretty girl. She's got nicer breasts than Arlette, fresher skin. But that's not what it takes.'

'Why did you try to make me believe that you'd only had sex with Arlette in the kitchen?'

He did not seem embarrassed.

'Have you been asking in all the hotels? I had to say that for my wife's sake. It would have hurt her unnecessarily. She always reckons that I'm going to drop her for a younger woman some day or another.'

'Would you have dropped her for Arlette?'

Fred looked Maigret in the eye.

'If she'd asked me, yes.'

'You were infatuated with her?'

'Call it what you like. I've had hundreds of women in my life, probably thousands. I never took the trouble to count. But I've never come across anyone like her.'

'Did you ask her to move in with you?'

'I gave her to understand that I wouldn't mind, and that it wouldn't be to her disadvantage.'

'She refused?'

Fred sighed, stared through his glass, then took a swig of his drink.

'If she hadn't refused, she'd probably still be alive. You know as well as I do that she had someone. I haven't been able to find out what kind of hold he had on her.'

'You tried?'

'I even followed her.'

'Without success?'

'She was craftier than me. What are you up to with the fairy?'

'You know Philippe?'

'No. But I know a few like him. Occasionally, some of them will venture into Picratt's, but I prefer to avoid that sort of clientele. Do you think it will pay off?'

It was Maigret's turn to respond with silence. Fred had worked it all out, obviously. He was almost in the same line of business. They both had a roughly similar approach, just different styles of working and different reasons for doing so.

'There are things you haven't told me about Arlette,' Maigret said quietly.

A faint smile played on Fred's lips.

'Have you guessed what they were?'

'I guessed what kind of things they were.'

'Might as well take advantage of my wife being upstairs. The kid may be dead, but I'd still rather not talk about her in front of Rose. Truth of it is, between you and me, I don't think I'll ever leave her. We are so used to each other that I couldn't do without her. Even if I'd gone off with Arlette, I'd probably have come back.'

The telephone rang. There was no booth. It was by the wash-basin in the toilets, and Maigret set off towards it saying, 'It's for me.'

He wasn't mistaken. It was Lapointe.

'You were right, chief. He immediately went straight to Doctor Bloch's. He took the bus. He was only up there a few minutes and came back out looking a bit paler. At the moment he's on his way to Place Blanche.'

'Is everything all right?'

'Everything's fine. Don't worry.'

Maigret went and sat back down. Fred didn't ask him anything.

'You were telling me about Arlette.'

'I always had a hunch she was a girl from a good family who had left home on a whim. As a matter of fact, it was Rose who first pointed certain things out to me that I hadn't noticed. I also had my suspicions that she was younger than she claimed. She'd probably swapped identity cards with an older friend.'

Fred spoke slowly, like a man mulling over pleasant memories. Before them, the long vista of the club in semi-darkness stretched like a tunnel, with the mahogany bar gleaming in the lamplight right at the end, near the door.

'It's not easy to explain what I meant. There are girls who've got a knack for love-making, and I've known some virgins who were more depraved than any old pro. Arlette was different. I don't know who the guy was who turned her out, but I take my hat off to him. I'm an expert, as I told you before, and when I say I've never met a woman like her, you can believe me. Not only did he teach her the lot, but I realized she knew things I did not know myself. At my age, imagine that. With the life I've led. I was stunned. And she got a kick out of it, I'd bet my life on it. Not just going to bed with anyone, but even her act, which I'm sorry you didn't see. I have known women of thirty-five or forty, most of them with a screw loose, who made a game of turning men on. And I've known little girls who played with fire. But never like her. Never so passionate. I'm not explaining it well, I know, but I can't describe exactly what I think. You asked about a man named Oscar. I don't know if he exists. I don't know who he is. What is for sure is that someone had a hold on Arlette, and he kept her on a tight rein. Do you think she suddenly had enough and ratted on him?'

'When she went to the Rue de La Rochefoucauld station at four in the morning, she was in no doubt that a crime would be committed and that it involved a countess.'

'Why did she say she had found that out here? Why did she claim to have overheard a conversation between two men?'

'For a start she was drunk. It was probably the drinking that prompted her to do it.'

'Or else she was drinking to get up enough courage to go through with it?'

'I wonder,' murmured Maigret, 'if how she was with young Albert . . .'

'Oh yes! I've found out he's one of your inspectors.'

'I didn't know either. He was really in love.'

'I noticed.'

'All women have some romantic feelings. He was dead-set on her starting a new life. She could have married him if she'd wanted to.'

'You think that made her feel disgusted with her Oscar?'

'At any rate she rebelled and went to the police. But she still didn't want to say too much. She left him a chance to get away with it, only giving a vague description and a first name.'

'It's still a dirty trick, don't you think?'

'Maybe, once she was face to face with the police, she regretted her impulse. She was surprised that they detained her and sent her to Quai des Orfèvres, and that gave her time to sleep off her champagne. After that she was much vaguer and virtually said she had made it all up.'

'That's just like a woman, I agree,' said Fred. 'What I wonder is how the guy found out. Because he was at Rue Notre-Dame-de-Lorette before her, waiting for her.'

Maigret looked at his pipe without saying a word.

'I bet,' Fred continued, 'you imagined I knew him and didn't want to say anything.'

'Maybe.'

'You even thought it was me for a while.'

It was Maigret's turn to smile.

'And there was I,' added Picratt's owner, 'wondering if the girl hadn't described someone a bit like me on purpose. Just because her man is completely different.'

'No. The description fits.'

'You know him?'

'His name is Oscar Bonvoisin.'

Fred didn't bat an eyelid. The name evidently meant nothing to him.

'He's good,' he said flatly. 'Whoever he is, I raise my hat to him. I thought I knew Montmartre inside out. I talked it over with the Grasshopper, who spends his time poking his nose into everything. Arlette had been working for me for two years. She lives a few hundred metres from here. As I told you, I sometimes followed her because I was curious. And after all that don't you think it's incredible that we don't know anything about this guy?'

He flicked the newspaper spread out on the table.

'He used to spend time with that crazy old countess too. Women like that don't go unnoticed. That's a very particular world, all that, where everybody knows everybody, more or less. But your men don't seem any more clued up than I am. Lognon came by just now and tried to pump me for information, but there isn't any.'

The telephone, again.

'Is that you, chief? I'm on Boulevard Clichy. He's just gone into the brasserie on the corner of Rue Lepic and done a round of the tables, as if he were looking for someone. He seemed disappointed. There is another brasserie next door, and first he stuck his face in the window. Then he went in and headed for the toilets. Janvier went in afterwards and questioned the bathroom attendant. Apparently he asked if someone called Bernard had left a message for him.'

'Did she say who Bernard is?'

'She claims not to know who he's talking about.'

A drug dealer, obviously.

'He's walking towards Place Clichy now.'

Maigret had barely hung up before the telephone rang again, and this time it was Torrence's voice.

'Hey, chief, going into the box room just now to air it out, I tripped over that guy Philippe's suitcase. We forgot to give it back to him. Do you think he's going to pick it up?'

'Not before he's found some drugs.'

When Maigret went back into the main room, Madame Rose and Arlette's young successor were both in the middle of the dance-floor. Fred had moved and was sitting in a booth like a customer. He motioned to Maigret to follow suit.

'We're rehearsing!' he declared with a wink.

The woman was very young, with a shock of blonde curls and a rosy complexion like a baby or a country girl. She had the sturdy build and naive expression to match.

'Shall I start?' she asked.

There was no music, no spotlights. Fred had just turned on an extra overhead above the dance-floor. He started humming the tune Arlette used to strip to, marking time with his hand.

Then Rose, after saying hello to Maigret, mimed to the young woman what she should do.

Awkwardly, the latter executed a series of what were supposed to be dance steps, swaying her hips as much as possible, and then, slowly, as she'd been taught, began to unbutton the long black sheath dress, which had been altered to fit her.

The look Fred gave Maigret spoke volumes. Neither of them laughed, and they tried not to smile. Her shoulders emerged from the material, then a breast, which it was a surprise to see naked in that setting.

Rose's hand indicated she should pause for a moment, and the girl kept her eyes fixed on it.

'Once all the way round the dance-floor . . .' ordered Fred, instantly resuming his humming. 'Not so fast . . . Tra la la la . . . Good!'

Then Rose's hand said:

'The other breast . . .'

Her nipples were large and pink. The dress slid slowly down, revealing the shadow of the navel, until finally, with a clumsy gesture, the girl let go of it entirely and stood naked in the middle of the dance floor, with both hands on her pubis.

'That will do for today,' Fred sighed. 'You can go and get dressed, sweetheart.'

She headed for the kitchen after picking up her dress. Rose sat with them for a minute.

'They'll just have to deal with it! I can't get any more out of her. She might as well be drinking a cup of coffee. It's nice of you to come and see us, inspector.'

She was sincere, meant what she said.

'Do you think you're going to find the murderer?'

'Monsieur Maigret is hoping to get his hands on him tonight,' announced her husband.

Looking at the two of them, she sensed she was interrupting and headed off for the kitchen herself, saying:

'I'm going to make something to eat. Will you have a bite with us, inspector?'

He did not say no. He was still in the dark, really. He had chosen Picratt's for its strategic location but also partly because he liked being there. When it came down to it, would young Lapointe have fallen in love with Arlette in another setting?

Fred went and turned off the lights round the dance-floor. They heard the young woman walking back and forth over their heads. Then she came downstairs and joined Rose in the kitchen.

'What were we saying?'

'We were talking about Oscar.'

'I suppose you've checked all the boarding houses?'

It was not even worth answering.

'And he didn't go to Arlette's place either?'

Their thoughts had come to the same point because they both knew the neighbourhood and its inhabitants' lives.

If Oscar and Arlette were intimately involved, they had to meet somewhere.

'She never got any telephone calls here?' asked Maigret.

'I didn't pay particular attention, but if it had happened regularly, I would have noticed.'

And she didn't have a telephone in the apartment either. According to the concierge, she didn't have male visitors, and that concierge was reliable, unlike the one on Rue Victor-Massé.

Lapointe had combed through the files on rented rooms, then Janvier had gone round them all and clearly made a conscientious job of it because he had picked up Fred's trail.

It was over twenty-four hours since Arlette's photograph had appeared in the newspapers, and no one so far had reported seeing her going anywhere regularly.

'I stand by what I said: he's good, that guy!'

It was evident from Fred's frown that he was thinking the same as Maigret: all in all, this Oscar didn't fall into any of the usual categories. He might easily live in the neighbourhood but he wasn't part of it.

It was futile, their attempts to place him, to imagine what kind of life he led.

He was a loner, as far as they could tell, and that impressed them both.

'Do you think he's going to try to do away with Philippe?'

'We'll know by tomorrow morning.'

'I went into the tabac on Rue de Douai just now. They're friends. I don't think anyone knows the neighbourhood as well as they do. Depending on the time of day, they get every type of customer you can think of in there. They don't have a clue either.'

'And yet Arlette met him somewhere.'

'At his place?'

Maigret would have sworn it wasn't there. Maybe this was all a bit ridiculous. The fact they knew almost nothing about him meant Oscar was assuming terrifying proportions. In spite of themselves, they were being influenced by the mystery in which he was veiled, perhaps crediting him with more intelligence than he actually possessed.

He was like a shadow, always more imposing than the object that casts it.

He was just a man after all, a man of flesh and blood, a former valet-chauffeur who had always been a womanizer.

The last time he had been seen in plain daylight was in Nice.

He had probably got the young chambermaid Antoinette Méjat pregnant, and she had died as a result, and slept with Maria Pinaco, who now was a prostitute on the streets.

Then, a few years later, he had bought a house near where he was born, which was clearly the behaviour of someone who has risen from lowly beginnings and suddenly has money. He was going back to the place of his birth to show his new fortune off to everyone who had witnessed his humble origins.

'Is that you, chief?'

The telephone, again. The traditional preamble. Lapointe was in charge of liaison.

'I'm calling from a little bar on Place Constantin-Pecqueur. He went into a block on Rue Caulaincourt and up to the fifth floor. He knocked on someone's door, but there was no answer.'

'What did the concierge say?'

'There's a painter who lives in the apartment, a sort of bohemian. She doesn't know if he shoots up, but she says he often looks strange. She's seen Philippe go up to his place before. He sometimes spends the night there.'

'Homosexual?'

'Probably. She thinks that such things don't exist, but she's never seen her tenant with a woman.'

'What's Philippe doing now?'

'He has turned right and is heading towards Sacré-Cœur.'

'Nobody seems to be following him?'

'Except us. Everything's going fine. It's starting to rain and it's freezing. If I'd known, I would've worn a sweater.'

Madame Rose had put a red checked tablecloth on the table, in the middle of which a soup tureen was steaming. Four places were laid, and the girl, who had changed into a navy-blue suit and looked very young, was helping her dish up. It was hard to imagine that a few minutes earlier she had been naked in the middle of the dance-floor.

'I'd be amazed if he never came here,' said Maigret.

'To see her?'

'When it came down to it, she was his pupil. I wonder if he was jealous.'

It was a question Fred could probably have answered better than he could, because Fred had also had women who slept with other men – women he even forced to sleep with other men – so presumably he knew the kind of feelings that could evoke.

'He won't have been jealous of the men she met here,' he said.

'You don't think?'

'Look, he must have felt sure of himself. He was convinced he'd got her and that she'd never leave.'

Was it the countess who had pushed her old husband off the terrace of The Oasis? Probably. If Oscar had committed the crime, he would not have had as much leverage over her. Even if they had been working together.

There was a certain irony to the whole story. The poor count was mad about his wife, pandering to her every whim, humbly begging her to leave a tiny space for him in her wake. But if he had loved her a little less, perhaps she would have put up with him. It was the very intensity of his passion that had made him hateful to her.

Had Oscar foreseen what would happen one day? Did he spy on the wife? Probably.

It was easy to picture the scene. The couple standing on the terrace after returning from the casino; the countess having no trouble manoeuvring the old man to the edge, then pushing him over.

She must have been scared afterwards to see the chauffeur calmly watching her, having witnessed the whole scene.

What had they said to each other? What deal had they struck?

At any rate, it wasn't the gigolos who had taken everything from her. A sizeable share of her fortune must have gone to Oscar.

He had had the good sense not to continue working for her. He had dropped out of sight and waited several years before buying a villa in the countryside where he was born.

He hadn't drawn attention to himself, hadn't splashed money around.

Maigret kept arriving at the same conclusion: this guy was a loner, and he had learned to be wary of loners.

Bonvoisin was a womanizer, they knew that, and the testimony of the old cook was telling. There must have been others before he met Arlette in La Bourboule.

Had he broken them in in the same way? Had he bound them on as tight a leash?

There hadn't been a whiff of scandal to expose him.

The countess had started falling to pieces, and no one had mentioned him.

She used to give him money, so he couldn't live far away, in the neighbourhood most probably, and yet a man like Fred, who had employed Arlette for two years, had never been able to find out a thing about him.

Who knew, perhaps it had been Oscar's turn to be smitten like the count? What was to say that Arlette hadn't tried to dump him?

She had tried it once, at least, after an impassioned conversation with Lapointe.

'What I don't understand,' said Fred, as if Maigret had been thinking aloud while eating his soup, 'is why he killed that crazy old girl. People are saying it was to get some jewellery that was hidden in her mattress. It's possible. Maybe it's a dead cert. But he had a hold on her and he could have got it some other way.'

'There's no reason to think she would have given her jewels up that easily,' said Rose. 'They were all she had left, and she must have been trying to make them last. Don't forget either that she was an addict, and they tend to shoot their mouths off.'

This was all Greek to Arlette's successor, and she looked curiously at each of them in turn. Fred had found her in a small theatre, where she had a walk-on part. She must have been bursting with pride finally to have her own act, but you could also feel that she was a little scared of going the same way as Arlette.

'Are you staying for tonight?' she asked Maigret.

'Possibly. I don't know.'

'He may leave in a few minutes or tomorrow morning, both are equally likely,' said Fred with a half-grin.

'If you ask me,' said Rose, 'Arlette was tired of him, and he felt it. A man can have a woman like her under his thumb for a while. Especially when she's very young. But she'd met other men . . .'

She looked rather insistently at her husband.

'Isn't that right, Fred? She had offers. Women aren't the only ones to have a feeling for things. I wouldn't be surprised if he'd decided to make a big score so he could take her to live somewhere else. His only mistake was to be too sure of himself and tell her. That's been other people's undoing too.'

All this was still confused, of course, but even so some truth was starting to emerge, with the disturbing figure of Oscar in particularly sharp relief.

Maigret went to answer the telephone yet again, but this time it was not for him. Someone on the other end of the line asked for Fred. The latter had the decency not to shut the door.

'Hello, yes . . . What? What are you doing there? Yes . . . He's here, yes . . . Don't shout so loud, you're deafening me . . . Fine . . . Yes, I know . . . Why? That's stupid, son . . . You're better off talking to him . . . That's right . . . I don't know what he will decide . . . Stay where you are . . . He'll probably come and find you . . .'

He was worried when he came back to the table.

'That was the Grasshopper,' he said, as if to himself.

He sat down but didn't immediately start eating again.

'I wonder what's going on in his head. It is true that in the five years he's worked for me, I've never known what he was thinking. He's never even told me where he lives. He could be married and have children, and it wouldn't surprise me.'

'Where is he?' asked Maigret.

'Right at the top of the Butte, Chez Francis, a bistro on the corner where there's always a guy with a beard who tells fortunes. Do you know the one I mean?'

Fred was thinking, trying to work something out.

'The funny thing is that Lognon, the inspector, is pacing up and down outside it.'

'Why's the Grasshopper up there?'

'He didn't spell it out. I gathered that it was to do with the guy called Philippe. The Grasshopper knows all the fairies in the neighbourhood . . . at one point I wondered if he wasn't one himself. He may also deal a bit of drugs in his spare time, just between you and me. I know you're not going to use it, and I swear he never does any in my place.'

'Is Philippe a regular at Chez Francis?'

'Seems that way. Maybe the Grasshopper knows more about it.'

'It still doesn't explain why he's there now.'

'All right! I'll tell you, if you haven't guessed already. But you've got to understand it's the Grasshopper's idea. He thinks that if we give you a tip-off, it can only stand us in good stead, because every now and then you'll remember it and turn a blind eye. In this business we've got to be on good terms with you. Besides, apparently he's not the only one who got the tip-off, because Lognon is skulking around up there too.'

When Maigret didn't stir, Fred exclaimed in surprise, 'You're not going?'

Then:

'I get it. Your inspectors need to call you here, and you can't make yourself scarce.'

Maigret headed to the telephone all the same.

'Torrence? Have you got any men there? Three? Good! Send them to Place du Tertre. They're to watch Chez Francis, the bistro on the corner. Tell the eighteenth to send men up that way too. I don't know exactly, no. I'm staying here.'

He slightly regretted making Picratt's his headquarters now, and was in two minds whether to get a car to drive him to the top of the Butte.

The telephone rang. It was Lapointe again.

'I don't know what he's doing, chief. For half an hour, he's been zigzagging round the streets of Montmartre. Maybe he suspects he's being followed and he's trying to shake us off. He went into a café on Rue Lepic, then back down to Place Blanche and did another circuit of the two brasseries. Then he retraced his steps and went back up

Rue Lepic. In Rue Tholozé he went into a building with a studio at the end of the courtyard. An old woman, who used to be a café-concert singer, lives there.'

'Is she a drug addict?'

'Yes. Jacquin went and questioned her as soon as Philippe left. She's the same sort as the countess, only shabbier. She was drunk. She started laughing and said she hadn't been able to give him what he was looking for. "I haven't even got any for myself!"'

'Where is he now?'

'He's having boiled eggs in a bar on Rue Tholozé. It's bucketing down with rain. Everything's fine.'

'He'll probably go up to Place du Tertre.'

'We almost did just now. But he suddenly turned round. I wish he'd make up his mind. My feet are cold.'

Rose and the new girl cleared the table. Fred fetched the bottle of brandy and filled two tasting glasses while the coffee was being poured.

'I'll have to go up and get dressed soon,' he announced. 'That's not me trying to get rid of you. Make yourself at home. Cheers.'

'You don't think the Grasshopper knows Oscar?'

'Well, well. I was just thinking that.'

'He's at the races every afternoon, isn't he?'

'And there's every chance that a man with nothing to do, like Oscar, is going to spend some of his time at the races. Is that what you mean?'

He emptied his glass, wiped his mouth, looked at the girl, who didn't know what to do with herself, and winked at Maigret.

'I'm going to get dressed,' he said. 'Come up for a second, sweetie, so I can talk to you about your act.'

After another wink, he added in a low voice:

'You've got to pass the time, eh?'

Maigret was left alone at the back of the club.

9.

'He went up to Place du Tertre, chief, and almost bumped into Inspector Lognon, who just had time to step back into the shadows.'

'You're sure he didn't see him?'

'Yes. He went and looked in the window of Chez Francis. Because of this weather there's hardly anyone there. A few regulars sitting glumly over their drinks. He didn't go in. Then he took Rue Mont-Cenis and went down the stairs. On Place Constantin-Pecqueur he stopped in front of another café. There's a big stove in the middle of the room, sawdust on the floor, marble tables, and the owner's playing cards with some locals.'

Picratt's new girl had come back down, a little embarrassed, and, not quite knowing where to put herself, had come and sat next to Maigret. Perhaps so as not to leave him on his own. She had already put on the black silk dress that had belonged to Arlette.

'What's your name?'

'Geneviève. They're going to call me Dolly. They're getting me photographed in this dress tomorrow.'

'How old are you?'

'Twenty-three. Did you see Arlette do her act? Is it true that she was incredible? I'm a bit clumsy, aren't I?'

Lapointe sounded glum next time he telephoned.

'He's going round in circles like a circus horse. We're following, and it's still bucketing down. We've gone back to Place Clichy and Place Blanche, where he did yet another circuit of the two brasseries. As he's got no drugs he's starting to have a little drink here and there. He can't find what he's looking for and he's walking more slowly, keeping in the shadow of the houses.'

'He doesn't suspect anything?'

'No. Janvier had a talk with Inspector Lognon. It was when he did another round of the addresses Philippe had gone to last night that Lognon heard about Chez Francis. He was just told that Philippe went there from time to time and that someone probably gave him drugs.'

'Is the Grasshopper still there?'

'No. He left a few minutes ago. At the moment Philippe's on his way back down the Rue du Mont-Cenis' stairs, I suppose so he can have a look in the café on Place Constantin-Pecqueur.'

Tania arrived with the Grasshopper. It wasn't time to turn Picratt's sign on yet, but they all must have been in the habit of coming early. Everyone felt the club was home, in a way. Rose looked in to cast an eye over the room before going up to get dressed. She still had a tea towel in her hand.

'There you are!' she said to the new girl.

Then, scrutinizing her from head to foot, she instructed, 'Next time don't put your dress on so early. It's a waste, the wear and tear.'

Finally, she said to Maigret, 'Help yourself, inspector. The bottle's on the table.'

Tania seemed out of sorts. She studied Arlette's successor and shrugged slightly.

'Shove up.'

Then she stared at Maigret for a long time.

'You haven't found him yet?'

'I'm hoping to tonight.'

'You don't think it might have occurred to him to make himself scarce?'

She knew something too. When it came down to it, they all knew some detail or other. He had already sensed that yesterday. Now Tania was wondering if it wouldn't be better for her if she talked.

'Did you meet him with Arlette?'

'I don't even know who he is or what he looks like.'

'But you know he exists?'

'I suspected as much.'

'What else do you know?'

'Where he hides, maybe.'

It was as if being cooperative was a matter of dishonour: she pouted as she talked, and it came out grudgingly.

'My dressmaker lives on Rue Caulaincourt, just opposite Place Constantin-Pecqueur. I usually go there about five in the afternoon, because I sleep most of the day. On two separate occasions I saw Arlette get off a bus at the corner of the square and walk across it.'

'Which way?'

'Towards the stairs.'

'Didn't you think of following her?'

'Why would I have done that?'

She was lying. She was curious. She probably hadn't been able to see anyone when she got to the bottom of the stairs.

'That's all you know?'

'That's it. He must live around there somewhere.'

Maigret had poured himself a glass of brandy and he lazily heaved himself to his feet when the telephone rang again.

'Same old story, chief.'

'The café on Place Constantin-Pecqueur?'

'Yes. He's only going there and the two brasseries on Place Blanche. He's looking in Chez Francis now.'

'Lognon is still at his post?'

'Yes. I've just seen him as I was going past.'

'Ask him from me to go to Place Constantin-Pecqueur and talk to the café owner. Not in front of the customers, if he can. I want him to ask if the owner knows Oscar Bonvoisin. If he says he doesn't, tell him to describe him, because they might know him under a different name.'

'Shall I do that now?'

'Yes. He's got time while Philippe makes his rounds. Tell him to call me immediately afterwards.'

When he went back into the main room, the Grasshopper was there, pouring himself a drink at the bar.

'You haven't caught him yet?'

'How did you get that tip-off about Chez Francis?'

'From some fairies. They all know each other, that lot. They told me about a bar on Rue Caulaincourt first, which Philippe goes to from time to time, and then about Chez Francis, where he sometimes goes late at night.'

'Do they know Oscar?'

'Yes.'

'Bonvoisin?'

'They don't know his last name. They said he was a local who comes every now and then and has a glass of white wine before going to bed.'

'Does he meet Philippe there?'

'Everyone talks to each other there. He's no different. Now, you can't say I haven't helped you.'

'He hasn't been seen today?'

'Or yesterday.'

'Did they tell you where he lives?'

'Somewhere local.'

Time was passing slowly now, and it felt a little as if it would all never end. Jean-Jean, the accordionist, arrived and went to the bathroom to clean his muddy shoes and run a comb through his hair.

'Is Arlette's murderer still on the loose?' he asked.

Then it was Lapointe on the telephone.

'I passed on your orders to Inspector Lognon. He is in Place Constantin-Pecqueur. Philippe has just gone into Chez Francis, where he is having a drink, but there's no one who matches Oscar's description there. Lognon will call you. I told him where you were. Was that right?'

Lapointe's voice had changed over the evening. He had to go into bars to telephone. This was his umpteenth call. He had probably had a little nip each time to warm himself up.

Fred came down, resplendent in his dinner-jacket, with a fake diamond stud in his starched shirt, his clean-shaven face pink and glowing.

'Go and get dressed,' he told Tania.

Then he went to turn on the lamps and spent a moment straightening the bottles behind the bar.

The second musician, Monsieur Dupeu, had just arrived when Maigret finally heard Lognon on the other end of the line.

'Where are you calling from?'

'From Chez Manière, on Rue Caulaincourt. I went to Place Constantin-Pecqueur. I've got the address.'

He was in a state of high excitement.

'Did you get it easily?'

'The owner fell for it completely. I didn't say I was with the police. I pretended that I had come up from the country and was looking for a friend.'

'Do they know him by his name?'

'They call him Monsieur Oscar.'

'Where does he live?'

'At the top of the stairs, on the right, a little house at the end of a small garden. There is a wall around it. The house isn't visible from the street.'

'Has he gone to Place Constantin-Pecqueur today?'

'No. They waited before starting the card game, because he's usually on time. That's why the owner took his place.'

'What has he told them he does?'

'Nothing. He doesn't talk much. They think he's a man of independent means who's got plenty of money. He is very good at belote. He often stops by in the morning about eleven o'clock, while he's doing his shopping at the market, to have a glass of white wine.'

'He does his shopping himself? He hasn't got a maid?'

'No. Or cleaning lady. They say he is a bit crazy.'

'Wait for me near the stairs.'

Maigret drained his glass and went and got his heavy, still wet overcoat from the cloakroom, while the two musicians played a few notes as if getting in the mood.

'Is it him?' asked Fred, still at the bar.

'Could be.'

'Will you come back this way for a drink or two?'

It was the Grasshopper who went and whistled for a taxi. As he shut the car door, he said under his breath:

'If it's the guy I've vaguely heard about, you'd better be careful. He'll kick.'

Water streamed down the taxi's windows, and the lights of the city were only visible through the fine cross-hatching of the rain. Philippe must be splashing around somewhere out there, with his escort of inspectors following in the shadows.

Maigret walked across Place Constantin-Pecqueur and found Lognon pressed against a wall.

'I've identified the house.'

'Any lights on?'

'I looked over the wall. You can't see anything. The fairy mustn't know the address. What's the plan?'

'Is there any way out at the back?'

'No. There's only this door.'

'We're going in. Are you armed?'

Lognon merely pointed at his pocket. There was a decrepit wall, like a wall in the country, with tree branches showing above it. Lognon set to work on the lock. It took him several minutes, while Maigret made sure no one was coming.

Once open, the door revealed a small garden, which looked like a parish priest's garden, and, at the end, a double-storey house of the sort you still find in some backstreets in Montmartre. No lights were on.

'Go and open the front door, then come back.'

Despite the lessons he had had with experts, Maigret had never been brilliant with locks.

'Wait for me outside and when the others come past, tell Lapointe or Janvier that I'm in here. They're to carry on following Philippe.'

There was no sound, no signs of life inside. Maigret had his gun in his hand all the same. It was hot in the hallway, and he caught a smell like something from the country. Bonvoisin must have wood fires. The house was damp. He thought twice about putting a light on, then shrugged and turned the switch he had found to his right.

Unexpectedly, the house was very clean, with none of that slightly cheerless and somehow dubious quality of most bachelors' homes. A coloured glass lantern lit the hall. He opened the door to his right and found himself in the sort of living room you see in window displays on Boulevard Barbès: crass but plush, with lots of heavy wood. The next room was a dining room from the same school, faux rustic with plastic fruit in a silver dish.

There wasn't a speck of dust anywhere, and when he went into the kitchen he saw it was equally meticulous. A small fire was still burning in the stove, and the water in the kettle was lukewarm. He opened the cupboards, found some bread, meat, butter, eggs and, in a scullery, some carrots, turnips and a cauliflower. The house couldn't have had a cellar, because there was a cask of wine in the scullery with an upturned glass on the bung, which suggested it saw regular use.

There was another room on the ground floor, across the corridor from the living room. It was a largish bedroom, with a bed covered with a satin eiderdown. Lamps with silk shades gave a very feminine light, and Maigret noted the abundance of mirrors, like in some brothels. There were almost as many mirrors in the adjoining bathroom.

Apart from the food in the kitchen, the wine in the scullery and the fire in the stove, there were no signs of life. Nothing lying around, as in even the best-kept houses. No ash in the ashtrays. No dirty washing or crumpled clothes in the wardrobes.

He understood why when he got to the first floor and opened both doors, not without a certain apprehension. Accentuated by the sound of rain on the roof, the silence was distinctly intimidating.

There was no one there.

The room on the left was Oscar Bonvoisin's actual bedroom, the one in which he lived his solitary life. The bed here was iron, with thick red blankets. It had not been made, and the sheets had seen better days. On the bedside table, there was some fruit, including a half-eaten apple that was already turning brown.

Dirty shoes and two or three packets of cigarettes lay around on the floor. There were cigarette butts more or less everywhere.

He may have had a proper bathroom downstairs, but here, in a corner of the room, there was only a basin with a single tap and dirty towels. A pair of men's trousers hung from a hook.

Maigret looked for papers without success. The drawers contained a hodgepodge of stuff, including cartridges for an automatic pistol, but not a single letter or personal document.

It was on the ground floor, when he went back downstairs, in the chest of drawers in the bedroom, that he discovered a drawer full of photographs. The film was in with them, along with the camera that had been used to take them and a magnesium lamp.

There weren't just photographs of Arlette. Twenty women at least, all young and good-looking, had modelled for Bonvoisin, who had got them all to assume the same sexual poses. Some of the photographs had been blown up. Maigret had to go back upstairs to find the cubbyhole on the first floor with a red lightbulb over some trays, and a mass of phials and powders.

He came back down when he heard footsteps outside and flattened himself against the wall, his gun pointed at the door.

'It's me, chief.'

It was Janvier, dripping with water, his hat bent out of shape by the rain.

'Have you found anything?'

'What's Philippe doing?'

'Going round in circles, same as before. I don't understand how he's still standing. He got in a conversation with a flower seller in front of the Moulin Rouge and asked her for drugs. She told me afterwards. She knows him by sight. He pleaded with her to tell him where he could find some. Then he went into a telephone box and called Doctor Bloch to tell him he was at the end of his rope and threaten him somehow. At this rate, we're going to have him throwing a fit on the pavement.'

Janvier looked at the empty house, with the lights on in every room.

'You don't think the bird has flown?'

His breath smelled of alcohol. He gave one of his tense little smiles, which Maigret knew well.

'You're not notifying the train stations?'

'Judging by the fire in the stove, he left the house at least three or four hours ago. In other words, if he means to make a run for it, he'll have got a train a long time ago. He's spoiled for choice.'

'We can still put the borders on alert.'

It was odd. Maigret felt no inclination to set all this heavy police machinery in motion. It was only a hunch, of course, but he thought this case could not spread beyond Montmartre, where everything had happened up until now.

'You think he's watching Philippe somewhere?'

Maigret shrugged. He did not know. He left the house and found Lognon pressed against the wall.

'You'd better turn off the lights and keep watch here.'

'Do you think he'll come back?'

He didn't think anything.

'Tell me, Lognon, where did Philippe go last night?'

The inspector had written the addresses in his notebook. After he was released, the young man had trailed lucklessly round all of them.

'You sure you haven't missed any out?'

Lognon bridled.

'I've told you everything I know. There is only one address left: his, on Boulevard Rochechouart.'

Maigret didn't say anything, just lit his pipe with a faint air of satisfaction.

'Good. Stay here, just in case. Follow me, Janvier.'

'Have you got an idea?'

'I think I know where we're going to find him.'

They set off on foot, hands jammed in pockets, overcoat collars turned up. It wasn't worth taking a taxi.

When they got to Place Blanche, they saw Philippe in the distance, coming out of one of the two brasseries and, closer to, young Lapointe in a cap, who nodded at them.

The other inspectors were not far away, still flanking the young man.

'You come with us too.'

It was only another 500 metres along the deserted boulevard. The nightclubs, their signs shining in the rain, could hardly be making a fortune in that weather. The doormen in their gold braid were firmly under cover, ready to unfurl their big red umbrellas.

'Where are we going?'

'Philippe's place.'

The countess had been killed in her apartment, hadn't she? And hadn't the murderer waited for Arlette in her place on Rue Notre-Dame-de-Lorette?

It was an old building. Over the closed shutters, they saw a sign for a picture framer and, to the right of the door, one for a bookseller. They had no choice but to ring the bell. The three men entered a dimly lit hallway, and Maigret gestured to his companions to keep quiet. Passing the concierge's lodge, he muttered an indistinct name, and all three started up the uncarpeted stairs.

There was light under a door on the first floor and a wet doormat. Then the automatic lighting went out, and it was dark until the sixth floor.

'Let me go first, chief,' whispered Lapointe, trying to squeeze between Maigret and the wall.

Maigret firmly pushed him away. He knew from Lognon that the maid's room Philippe lived in was third on the left on the top floor. His electric torch showed the narrow, yellowing corridor was empty, and he pressed the light switch.

Then he stationed his men either side of the third door and put one hand on the door knob while holding his gun in the other. The knob turned. The door wasn't locked.

He pushed it with his foot, then froze, listening. As in the house he had just left, all he could hear was the rain on the roof and the water running in the pipes. It seemed as if he could hear his companions' heartbeats too, or maybe they were his own.

He reached out his hand, found the switch by the doorframe.

There was nobody in the room. There was no wardrobe to hide in. Bonvoisin's upstairs bedroom was a palace compared to this one. The bed didn't have sheets. A chamber pot hadn't been emptied. Dirty laundry lay on the floor.

Lapointe bent down unnecessarily to look under the bed. There wasn't a living soul in that room. It stank.

Suddenly Maigret had a feeling that something had moved behind him. To the amazement of the two inspectors, he jumped backwards and, as he turned, slammed his shoulder into the door opposite.

The door gave. It wasn't locked. There was someone behind it, someone watching them, and Maigret had noticed the door move imperceptibly.

His momentum threw him forward into the room, and he would have fallen over if he hadn't collided with a man almost as heavily built as him.

The room was dark, and it was Janvier who had the sense to turn on the light.

'Watch out, chief . . . .'

Maigret had already been headbutted in the chest. He staggered backwards, still without falling, and reached for something that toppled over, a bedside table with a piece of pottery on it that smashed.

Grabbing his gun by the barrel, he tried to hit his assailant with the butt. He did not know this Oscar they had all been talking about but he recognized him now, from other people's descriptions and the picture he had of him in his imagination. The man had crouched down again and was barrelling towards the two inspectors who were blocking his way.

Lapointe instinctively clung on to his jacket while Janvier tried to grab hold of him.

They could barely see each other. There was a body lying on the bed, but they didn't have time to attend to it.

Janvier was knocked down, and Lapointe was left holding the jacket, as a figure raced off into the corridor. Then a shot rang out. They didn't know who had fired at first. It was Lapointe, who didn't dare look in the man's direction and stared at his gun in a sort of stupor.

Bonvoisin had gone a few more paces, bent double, then collapsed on the floor in the corridor.

'Watch out, Janvier.'

He was holding an automatic. They could see the barrel moving. Then, slowly, the fingers opened and the gun rolled on to the ground.

'You think I killed him, chief?'

Lapointe's eyes were bulging, his lips trembling. He could not believe that he had done that and he looked at his gun again with amazed respect.

'I killed him!' he repeated, without daring to look at the body.

Janvier bent down to it.

'Dead. You got him bang in the middle of the chest.'

Maigret thought that Lapointe was going to faint for a moment and put his hand on his shoulder.

'Is that your first?' he asked quietly.

Then, to cheer him up:

'Don't forget that he killed Arlette.'

'That is true . . .'

183

It was strange to see Lapointe's childlike expression. He didn't know whether to laugh or cry.

They heard cautious footsteps on the stairs. A voice asked:

'Is someone hurt?'

'Stop them coming up,' Maigret told Janvier.

He had to attend to the figure he had glimpsed on the bed. It was a girl of sixteen or seventeen, the bookseller's maid. She wasn't dead, but she had been gagged with a towel to make sure she didn't scream. Her hands were tied behind her back, and her blouse was hitched up to her armpits.

'Go down and ring the Police Judiciaire,' Maigret told Lapointe. 'If there's a bistro still open, make the most of it and have a drink.'

'Really?'

'It's an order.'

It was some time before the girl was able to talk. She had got back to her room around ten o'clock at night after going to the cinema. A stranger was waiting for her in the dark. He grabbed her before she had time to switch on the light and jammed the towel in her mouth. Then he tied her hands and threw her on the bed.

He ignored her at first, listening to the sounds of the building and opening the door to the corridor a crack every now and then.

He was waiting for Philippe, but he was wary, and took care not to wait in his room. He had probably looked into it before going into the maid's room, hence the open door.

'What happened then?'

'He undressed me, and because my hands were tied he had to tear my clothes off.'

'He raped you?'

She nodded and started crying. Picking up some light-coloured material from the floor, she said, 'My dress is ruined . . .'

She did not realize that she had had a narrow escape. There was every chance that Bonvoisin wouldn't have let her live. Like Philippe, she had seen him. Probably the only reason he had not strangled her sooner, like the two other women, was because he wanted to keep having his fun with her until the young man got back.

At three in the morning the body of Oscar Bonvoisin was lying in a metal drawer in the Forensic Institute, not far from the bodies of Arlette and the countess.

After Philippe had got into a fight with an addict in Chez Francis, which he had finally gone into, he had been taken to the nearest station by a uniformed officer. Torrence had gone to bed. The inspectors who had gone in circles from Place Blanche to Place du Tertre, and from there to Place Constantin-Pecqueur, had gone home too.

Leaving the Police Judiciaire with Lapointe and Janvier, Maigret hesitated, then suggested:

'What about a drink?'

'Where?'

'Picratt's.'

'I'm out,' said Janvier. 'My wife's waiting for me, and the baby's going to wake us up early.'

Lapointe didn't say anything, but he got into the taxi after Maigret.

They reached Rue Pigalle in time to see the new girl do her act. When they walked in, Fred came over.

'Is it him?'

Maigret nodded, and, a few moments later, a champagne bucket appeared on their table, which, as chance would have it, was number six. The black dress moved slowly down the milky white body of the girl, who was watching them nervously. She hesitated before exposing her stomach and, as she had done earlier, when she was finally naked, she covered her sex with both hands.

Did Fred do it on purpose? He should have switched the spotlight off at that moment and left the room in darkness long enough for the dancer to pick up her dress and hold it up in front of her. But the spotlight stayed on, and the poor girl, not knowing which way to turn, finally decided to flee to the kitchen, revealing a round white behind.

The scattering of customers burst out laughing. Maigret thought Lapointe was laughing too, but then, when he looked, he saw that the inspector was crying as though his heart would break.

'I'm sorry,' he stammered. 'I shouldn't . . . I know it's stupid. But I . . . I loved her, you see!'

He was even more ashamed when he woke up the next morning, because he couldn't remember how he had got home.

His sister, who was very cheery – Maigret had coached her – sang out as she opened the curtains:

'So, this is how you let the detective chief inspector put you to bed, is it?'

That night Lapointe had buried his first love. And killed his first man. As for Lognon, no one had remembered to relieve him of his watch, and he was still languishing on the steps in Place Constantin-Pecqueur.

OTHER TITLES IN THE SERIES